Emily Harvale lives in Ea̶ although she would pref Alps...or Canada...or any̶ months of snow. Emily loves snow almost as much as she loves Christmas.

Having worked in the City (London) for several years, Emily returned to her home town of Hastings where she spends her days writing. And wondering if it will snow.

You can contact her via her website, Twitter, Facebook or Instagram.

There is also a Facebook group where fans can chat with Emily about her books, her writing day and life in general. Details are on the 'For You' page of Emily's website.

Author contacts:
www.emilyharvale.com
www.twitter.com/emilyharvale
www.facebook.com/emilyharvalewriter
www.instagram.com/emilyharvale

***

Scan the code above to see all Emily's books on Amazon

Also by this author

The Golf Widows' Club
Sailing Solo
Carole Singer's Christmas
Christmas Wishes
A Slippery Slope
The Perfect Christmas Plan
Be Mine
It Takes Two
Bells and Bows on Mistletoe Row

Lizzie Marshall series:
Highland Fling – book 1
Lizzie Marshall's Wedding – book 2

The Goldebury Bay series:
Ninety Days of Summer – book 1
Ninety Steps to Summerhill – book 2
Ninety Days to Christmas – book 3

The Hideaway Down series:
A Christmas Hideaway – book 1
Catch A Falling Star – book 2
Walking on Sunshine – book 3
Dancing in the Rain – book 4

Hall's Cross series
Deck the Halls – book 1
The Starlight Ball – book 2

Michaelmas Bay series
Christmas Secrets in Snowflake Cove – book 1
Blame it on the Moonlight – book 2

ISBN 978-1-909917-59-0

Published by Crescent Gate Publishing

Print edition published worldwide 2020
E-edition published worldwide 2020

Editor Christina Harkness

Cover design by JR and Emily Harvale

A Wedding

at

Wynter House

Emily Harvale

The Dedication below was written by one of the lovely members of my Readers' Club, to someone very special in her life.

~

This book is dedicated to Peter.
You are my rock in rough seas, my light in the dark, my joy in times of sadness. My love, my life, my husband and my best friend.
Love always,
June xx

Chapter One

'You cannot possibly be serious. I simply do not believe it. Are you intent on killing me? Is that it?'

Olivia's bony right hand shot to her chest, her breath came in gasps and her eyes resembled those of a goldfish Rafe had won at the Merriment Bay Summer Fayre when he was seven. It was a day he still remembered fondly although it was more than thirty years ago. Thirty-two years, in fact. A rare day out with his mother and father, just a few short weeks before he was shipped off to boarding school in Scotland.

'He's serious,' his brother said, an odd smirk hovering on his lips.

Olivia stared from Rafe to Adam and back again, her mouth agape as the fingers of her left hand clenched the curve of the armrest. She shivered visibly despite being seated merely inches from a roaring fire in her private sitting room in Wynter House.

'No.' Olivia lowered her hand from her chest and thumped it on the other armrest. 'This must be some sort of ill-conceived joke. It must be.'

Rafe shook his head and sighed loudly. He had broken the news as gently and rationally as he could, but the truth was, he could hardly believe it himself, so he hadn't expected his grandmother to accept it without question.

It had been bad enough telling her, only two days earlier, that he and Adam had met their half-sister, Catherine and their niece, Kyra at The Mane Event. Olivia had been less than pleased to hear of the meeting, and the fact that it had happened at Neva's salon seemed to exacerbate what Olivia had made abundantly clear was an undesirable occurrence. But at least she hadn't had another heart attack.

He had seriously considered keeping this latest turn of events in the Wynter and Devon lives, a secret, in case this revelation did. But whilst he had been able to keep certain things from Olivia until he was ready to disclose them, for example, the gin distillery in the Old Barn, he knew he couldn't keep this from her. Everyone in Merriment Bay, at Wynter House, and far beyond would be talking about it before too long and it might even make the news. Olivia now spent most of her day in her own rooms, reading books and newspapers, or listening to the radio. As distasteful as he knew she would find it, there had been no choice but to break it to her.

'Unfortunately, it's true. As bizarre as it may seem. It's not a joke, and killing you is the last thing any of us wants to do. If I could have kept it from you, believe me, I would've done so. But things like this always come out.'

'Always come out? You say that as if such things were an everyday occurrence. I've never heard of anything like it in my entire life. Are you honestly telling me that there may be a woman's body buried beneath the floor of a hitherto unknown cellar in Devon Villa and that a handwritten confession dating from the 1800s states that a member of the Devon family was her murderer?'

Rafe nodded. No matter how many times he'd thought about this in the last hour or so since receiving the phone call from Cat, it didn't seem any less crazy.

'Yes. Cat, Kyra and Mary have all moved out, temporarily. The police were there last night and again today, and will decide whether or not there'll be a criminal investigation. To do that, the body needs to be dated. But as the confession indicates the body is that of Jerusalem Raine who went missing in the summer of 1826, it's likely the police won't pursue the matter further. The coroner will be involved and there may be an inquest. But until the specialists dig up the cellar floor and find out if it's true, there's nothing we can do. We're hoping it'll only come to the attention of the local media but it may go national.'

'Go national!' Olivia's shriek set Rafe's teeth on edge. 'An inquest! I must be having a nightmare. This cannot be real.'

'It's real.' Adam's tone held a hint of amusement and Olivia looked daggers at him and at Rafe.

'I have no idea why you are able to find the slightest bit of levity in this situation, Adam. And as for you, Rafe, the fact you've welcomed the Devon girl and her offspring into this family is enough to make us front page news. Now you're telling me that we'll be seeing the word 'murder' linked to our name because of them. I cannot take this in. Where's that damn nurse when I need her?'

Olivia cast an infuriated glance around the room as she took several deep, dramatic breaths, but the healthy glow in her cheeks and the icy look in her eyes made it clear she was in no danger of needing medical attention.

Adam smirked and raised his brows with a look of mild contempt. 'If you mean Hazel, she's no longer your nurse. You made it perfectly clear that you didn't want her around. Either as a nurse or my girlfriend.'

Olivia glared at him and pointed one long finger. 'That was half the problem. She spent most of her time flirting with you. Although I accept that she did save your life, so I'm grateful to her for that. But now she's got her claws in you and you seem to think you owe her something.'

'That's not the case at all. And that's not what happened. Apart from her saving my life. I was the one doing all the chasing. Hazel was professional throughout. I'm not with her out of gratitude, Olivia.'

'Hasn't she got a home of her own to go to?'

'Yes she has. But I asked her to stay here until she gets her next assignment. I know you find this difficult to comprehend – and to be honest, so do I, but I'm with Hazel because I fell in love.'

'Nonsense. You and Rafe have both been swept off your feet by scheming women and the sooner the pair of you see sense, the better.'

'That's enough.' Rafe's tone silenced them. 'I've told you, Olivia that I won't have you saying unpleasant things about my girlfriend. Or Adam's. And we seem to have veered off the subject we came to discuss. Let's stop bickering and get back to that, shall we?'

Adam shrugged. 'Until we hear more from Cat, I'm not sure there's anything else to be said about it, is there?'

'I assume you're stopping the tours and closing the house to paying guests,' Olivia snapped.

'I haven't re-opened it as yet,' Rafe said. 'I wasn't sure how long it would take until you were fully recovered from your heart attack, and then when Adam fell ill, I decided not to take the risk. I was hoping we might re-open to visitors in mid-to late February, but now that our Wyntersleap Gin is really taking off, and what with everything else going on, I've set the opening date for the end of March. I asked Gavin to post notices at the gates and Judith to do so on the website, and we've either refunded tickets purchased for February 1st onwards, or given credit notes for a later date to any who had booked tours. We've said it's due to renovation work being carried out in the house and gardens. We rarely see many visitors prior to Easter in any event so that gives us time. It also means the cottages in the village may be ready. The repairs and redecoration will begin shortly and once everyone is back in their own homes, life here can return to normal.'

'Life will never be normal again now that you've brought the Devons to our door.'

'You're exaggerating, Olivia.' Rafe shook his head and smiled. 'But perhaps we'll have a new normal. I think life is going to become more exciting from here on out.'

'That's one word for it, I suppose. But how will all this scandal affect your new business venture? Have you considered that?'

'Of course. I don't think it'll make any

difference. Even Amelia felt it wasn't an issue.'

'That was before they found a body in that family's cellar and discovered you're related to a murderer.'

Rafe stiffened. 'Again, Olivia. Not an issue in my opinion.'

'If anything,' Adam said, grinning. 'I think it may boost sales of Rafe's gin. We could even make more of it and say something like, 'People have been fighting for our gin recipe for centuries'. Well, perhaps not that, but something along those lines.'

Rafe raised his brows. 'You heard Cat say that the body is believed to be that of Jerusalem Raine, the daughter of a previous vicar of St Mary-in-the-Fields, didn't you? I'm not sure we should be making jokes about it.' But he grinned at Adam anyway.

'That's true I suppose.' Adam looked a little disappointed.

'And it's not *my* gin, Adam. It's Sean's and the Wyntersleap Inn's as well as yours and mine. I do think we may have to delay the official launch though. Amelia wanted it to be on Valentine's Day, but we've postponed it temporarily. I'm wondering if, perhaps, we should wait a few more weeks, what with everything going on. Not because of any potential scandal, more because of the time element involved. I'm simply not sure we'd be able to get everything in place until late

February. We still haven't finalised the brochure, having decided not to take the route Amelia had planned, but thanks to her contacts in the City, we're already getting orders. To be honest, we'd struggle to complete them if we had to spend an inordinate amount of time preparing for a launch event.'

'You shouldn't have sacked Amelia,' Olivia said. 'She could have handled the launch seamlessly. Oh, I know you and that public house landlord partner of yours wanted to take your brand in a different direction from the immensely profitable one Amelia was suggesting. Which I think you'll all come to regret in time. But you could have retained her expert services and let her improve upon the path you want to take.'

'Letting Amelia go is one thing I'm certain I won't regret. Perhaps we should see how this latest development plays out for a day or two before making any new decisions. And Adam said, until we hear from Cat, there's really nothing else we can do. We could stand here and speculate, but what's the point in that?' Rafe met Olivia's icy stare. 'Except to add that we've invited Cat and Kyra for Sunday lunch.'

Olivia looked even more horrified.

'Here? You've invited those people here for Sunday lunch?'

'Yes.' Rafe suppressed his irritation and forced a smile. 'Cat and Kyra are both looking forward to meeting you. Catherine prefers to be called Cat. But I'm sure she'll tell you that herself.'

'Cat.' Olivia gave a derisive snort. 'Why am I surprised?' She shook her head and raised her chin defiantly. 'I'm not certain I'll be well enough to come down.'

'I thought you might say that. Amias Wells will be joining us. He and Cat are dating.'

Olivia glared at him in disbelief. 'Amias Wells? Alwick's boy?'

'Yes.'

'Dear God. Can this fiasco get any worse? First you allow the villagers and other riff raff to run riot through this house, then you acknowledge those people as relations and now you're inviting thieves into our home.'

'Olivia! The Wells family are not thieves. Amias is our friend and I'd like you to remember that. Cat and Kyra are our relatives. The villagers are always welcome, and if, by riff raff, you're referring to Neva and her family, please never use that reference again.'

'You're entitled to your opinion and I'm entitled to mine.'

'Then please keep your opinions to yourself. Mary Devon will also be joining us.'

'Mary Devon!' Olivia's knuckles turned white as she gripped the arms of her chair and glowered at him. 'Now you really must be joking. If you think for one moment I'll allow that harlot under my roof, you can think again.'

'I'm not joking. And I hate to remind you, but this is not your roof. It's my roof. And I've invited Mary Devon. If you can't bring yourself to be civil then I agree that it's best if you stay in your rooms. But you are going to have to meet Cat and Kyra at some stage. Whether you like it or not, Olivia, they are Wynters and they're your flesh and blood. Furthermore, I'm telling Cat that she and Kyra are welcome at Wynter House and that they should consider it their home.'

'Your father will be turning in his grave.'

'I doubt that very much. I think, if he had lived, he would've eventually acknowledged the relationship and made his daughter and granddaughter welcome. I hope you'll give the matter serious thought and choose to do the same. Cat is your granddaughter, Olivia, and Kyra, your great-granddaughter. They are both kind, friendly and talented people, not to mention, beautiful. In some ways, they both remind me of you. Forget your pride and meet them. I'm sure you'll be glad if you do.'

Olivia held his gaze for a second or two before turning her head and staring intently into the flames.

'I'd sooner burn in hell.'

'I think that's already been arranged,' Adam said, smiling sardonically.

Rafe bit back a laugh and both he and

Adam turned to leave.

There was no point in talking to Olivia when she was in this frame of mind.

Chapter Two

'How did she take it?' Neva asked, meeting Rafe in the hall so that they could have lunch together. She had spent the morning at Wynter House, a rare event on a week-day since she and Jo had moved into the flat in Merriment Bay and started renovating their salon. But they had agreed on a trompe l'oeil for one of the salon walls, and Cat and Kyra had agreed to paint it. It was to be similar to Botticelli's famous painting of Venus rising from the waves, and although they'd seen several images of the painting on the internet, Rafe had said there were a couple of books on Botticelli's work in his library, so having spent the night, as she often did, Neva had stayed on to look through the books. Rafe had come to find her shortly after receiving the phone call from Cat about the body in the cellar, and Neva had remained at Wynter House to offer Rafe some support. Not that he needed it. It was more that Neva wanted to know how Olivia would react.

Rafe gave her a wan smile and slid an arm around her, pulling her close and looking her directly in the eye.

'Exactly as we'd expected.'

'That good, huh?' Neva cocked her head to one side and grinned up at him. 'I'm sure she'll come round in time. She's only a Wynter by marriage but the family means the world to her. I've learnt that much since I came here. Cat and Kyra are Wynters by blood and they're her son's daughter and granddaughter. She can't ignore that, can she? She'll have to accept them into the fold even if it kills her.'

'In theory, yes. But with Olivia, there's no telling what she'll do. She can be as stubborn as a mule. This latest revelation hasn't exactly endeared the Devons to her, and she already blames Mary for leading my father astray. Not that he took much leading. In fact, he was probably the one doing that, if I'm honest.'

'But she can hardly blame Cat or Kyra for the fact that Mary and your dad had an affair for years. They're innocent victims really.'

'They're Devons. And both are illegitimate. Cat wasn't married to Kyra's father. It doesn't matter to me but it matters to Olivia. And neither was she best pleased about Cat and Amias dating. Welcoming the Devons with open arms is going to be a stretch. Including the Wells family into that is never going to happen.'

'If Cat and Amias marry, she'll have no choice. And from seeing them together and hearing the story about how they've loved one another all their lives since they first met, I think it's a pretty sure bet they're going to get married, don't you?'

Rafe kissed her on her nose and nodded, tipping his head to one side as if something had suddenly occurred to him.

'Get a room, you lovebirds.'

Neva recognised Ethel's voice, and Queenie's laugh and glanced over her shoulder, grinning at them. They were heading towards the dining room, Ethel without her teeth, as always and looking as if she had fallen into a bag of old clothes and come out wearing a dress three sizes too big and two cardigans. Queenie was immaculately dressed, as usual and her two corgis, Boris and Duchess were trotting regally behind.

'Don't worry, Rafe,' Queenie said, smiling at him. 'I'm not taking my little ones into lunch. George said he would take them for a run and have his lunch after we've had ours.'

Rafe had relaxed his rule about having pets in the house almost as soon as everyone had arrived at Wynter House way back before Christmas, but several rooms remained off-limits and the dining room was one of them.

Rafe smiled back. 'I'm glad to hear it.'

'Is it true that there's a woman's body in a

hidden cellar in Devon Villa?' Ethel asked. She was never one to beat about the bush.

Rafe's brows shot up. 'How on earth did you hear about that? I only found out myself about an hour or so ago.'

'Walls have ears.' Ethel tapped her nose for some reason.

Queenie moved closer. 'Cecil and Ronnie happened to be passing Olivia's suite of rooms while taking Persephone for her walk and they couldn't help but overhear a sentence or two.'

'Pah,' Ethel said, chuckling. 'We all know they stood outside and listened.'

'Was the woman really murdered?' Queenie opened her eyes wide as she whispered, 'murdered'.

Ethel gave her a slap on the arm. 'Of course she was murdered. Decent folk don't bury their dead in their cellars, then board the cellars up. I can't wait to find out all about it.' She grinned at Rafe. 'Perhaps your sister and her family will have some news when they come to Sunday lunch.'

Rafe furrowed his brows. 'How do you know they're coming to? ... Oh. Cecil and Ronnie overheard that as well, I suppose.'

Neva grinned even though it wasn't funny. At least Rafe had told all his guests, together with the staff at Wynter House about his sister and his niece, which meant there were no rumours flying around about that relationship.

Although when he told everyone at dinner on Wednesday night that he and Adam had now met Cat and Kyra, quite a few comments had been made. Cecil and Ronnie, in particular asked several questions, all of which Rafe answered as honestly but as vaguely as possible.

Ethel nodded. 'They heard every last word. You should learn to close doors, young Rafe. I'm starving. I hope Penny and Taryn have made something nice for lunch. I could murder steak and kidney pie.'

'Steak and kidney pie?' Queenie screwed up her face as she and Ethel strolled past Neva and Rafe. 'Kidneys are only fit for dogs to eat. When was the last time you had steak and kidney pie?'

'When Wendy made it for me at the Wyntersleap Inn, the week before Christmas. You had it too. But I told you it was steak and mushroom and you didn't even notice.'

Queenie gasped in horror and Ethel cackled in delight. George came along the hall to meet them, no doubt to take Boris and Duchess for their run, and Ethel asked him if he'd heard about the body.

Rafe sighed and shook his head, but he was smiling as he led Neva towards the dining room.

'I'll miss them when they move back to the village. Although I won't miss Cecil and

Ronnie. I really should have another word with them about eavesdropping.'

'It's a waste of breath. They simply can't help themselves.'

And it was true. They couldn't.

They eavesdropped again when Cat, Kyra, Amias and Mary came to Wynter House for Sunday lunch – although on that occasion Rafe had closed the door and it was only later, when everyone sat together for afternoon tea, and for Cat and Kyra to be 'formally introduced' to the rest of the guests and staff at Wynter House, that Cecil casually mentioned a snippet or two he and Ronnie had overheard.

Olivia had sent word, via her personal assistant, Judith that she felt too unwell to come down either for lunch or for afternoon tea. A fact that pleased Neva far more than it pleased either Rafe or Adam. Cat and Kyra seemed both disappointed and relieved not to be meeting their grandmother and great-grandmother, respectively and Neva agreed it was a pity, inwardly thanking all that was holy for keeping Olivia and the woman's unkind comments from potentially ruining a wonderful day.

And it had been wonderful.

Cat was clearly emotional when she first entered Wynter House and said how beautiful it was.

Rafe had beamed with pride. 'This house is

also your home. You're welcome here at any time, whether it's for a brief visit, or to come here to stay. Wynter House is, and always will be, home to the Wynter family. And to their loved ones, of course.' He smiled at Amias and Mary.

'Wow!' Kyra said. 'I might take you up on that one day.'

'Please do,' Rafe said, and Neva could see he meant it.

Adam confirmed it. 'You are family, and Wynter House is your ancestral home.'

Cat looked unsure. 'You might not want us here when all this latest stuff comes out and everyone in Merriment Bay starts gossiping. Or if there are reporters banging on your door.'

Adam grinned. 'I hate to say this, but you're the ones who'll be bearing the brunt of most of the gossip now that the body of Jerusalem Raine has been "discovered" in your cellar.'

Kyra laughed, perhaps a little nervously. 'We may need somewhere to hide out from the press. I like the thought of having an ancestral home to run to.'

Rafe laughed too. 'This is the perfect place to do that. They can't set foot on the drive, and if they do, Carruthers here will soon show them the error of their ways, won't you, Archie?'

Carruthers, who had clearly been given strict instructions by Olivia to dress the part today, stepped forward and gave a small bow as Rafe introduced him. He wore formal dress – a white, wing collar dress shirt, black morning coat and matching tie, grey waistcoat and grey, pinstriped trousers, along with his white gloves.

'I most certainly shall, Mr Rafe,' he said, raising one eyebrow and lowering the other in his usual manner.

Adam laughed and confirmed the formal attire was due to Olivia's insistence.

'Carruthers is usually a little more casual. Although not much. Olivia believes in all the pomp, but even Carruthers believes there are certain standards to uphold. Don't you?'

Carruthers gave a brief smile, his eyebrows rising and falling again as Adam patted him on the shoulder.

'Indeed there are, Mr Adam. It's an honour to meet you, Miss Catherine and Miss Kyra.' He gave them both a little bow of his head.

Cat gave him a friendly smile. 'We're delighted to meet you. But please just call us, Cat and Kyra.'

Neva laughed. 'Good luck with that.'

She gave Carruthers a jovial apology and explained to Cat and Kyra that Carruthers struggled with such informality. He returned her smile, together with a nod.

'Let's have some drinks,' Adam said, wrapping his arm around Hazel's waist. 'I'm dying to hear all about Jerusalem Raine and how you came to find her body in your cellar.'

Mary shivered. 'Please don't remind us of that. I'm definitely going to have to sell the house.'

'Because of the body in the cellar?' Neva glanced from Mary to Rafe and back again.

'Yes. But it's not only because of this latest tragedy. It just doesn't feel the same now that Mother's gone. And everywhere I look I'm reminded of Jeremy Stone, mainly due to the fact that all the work he started has been left unfinished, and my en suite is more like a building site than a place of sanctuary. Oh! I'm sorry. I have no idea why I brought that up.'

Neva shot her a comforting smile. 'I happen to know a good builder. And he happens to live next door to you.'

'Dennis is wonderful, and I must confess, Catherine, Kyra and I have already discussed that possibility.' Mary smiled, but it didn't reach her eyes. She went on to say that no matter what, she didn't feel she could remain in Devon Villa. It wasn't just because of the body in the cellar. It was also because her mother was no longer there.

And that gave Neva an idea.

'Will you buy somewhere else, or are you intending to stay with Cat and Amias?'

Amias' face dropped but he quickly recovered himself and said that Mary was welcome to stay for as long as she liked.

'Don't worry, Amias,' Mary said, and told them she had other plans, mentioning briefly that a bungalow a few doors away from a friend of hers was coming up for sale and that she was considering selling Devon Villa. 'I'll have to hope that the gruesome discovery in the cellar doesn't put off potential buyers.'

Neva struggled to contain her excitement. 'If you're really serious about selling Devon Villa, I may know someone who'll be interested to buy. Sorry to do your sister out of the commission, Amias, but we're hoping my sister Rowan and her family will move to Merriment Bay. They've said they'd like to but suitable properties are few and far between. Devon Villa would be the perfect house for them. Nigel's a builder. Rowan loves Edwardian houses. Finding a body in the cellar won't bother them. It'll be an added attraction as far as my niece, Sasha is concerned. I know they'll make you a really good offer.'

Mary and Cat exchanged glances and smiles.

'It seems that everything may work out well for quite a few of us,' Cat said, but she advised her mum to give it careful consideration. 'You've lived in Devon Villa all your life. Selling up shouldn't be done lightly. It'll be a big upheaval.'

Mary didn't appear to be swayed. 'Change

is often the best medicine, so they say. So many of us here are starting afresh. Why shouldn't I be one of them?'

And as much as Neva was enjoying the day, she couldn't wait for an opportunity to ring her sister, Rowan and give her the potentially brilliant news. She'd include her Mum and Dad in the video call. She longed to see the excitement on their faces.

Rafe must have read her mind. He leant in to whisper in her ear.

'I know it's your dream come true, but don't get all your hopes up until Mary's made her final decision. People often change their minds.'

'I know.' Neva smiled at him. 'I'll tell them it's not definite. But I have a really good feeling about this, Rafe.'

And she did. Somehow she was sure that Rowan, Nigel, Sasha and Tempest would be moving into Devon Villa within a matter of months.

Could life get any better than this?

Chapter Three

Jo was feeling sorry for herself – and she didn't like that one bit. After all, what did she have to moan about?

She'd got out of a doomed engagement. OK, Rob had broken up with her before she got a chance to break up with him. That was a bit annoying. But the result was the same. She'd wanted out, and she was out.

She'd been saved from living her life in Upminster. It was a lovely place, but it wasn't London, and it certainly wasn't Merriment Bay. Moving here had been the best thing to happen to her.

Well, maybe not the best thing. Buying a flat in London with Neva ten years ago was the best.

Or now being in business with Neva right here in Merriment Bay. Perhaps that was the best thing?

No. Being Neva's best friend was the best thing. They had been best friends their entire lives, and regardless of the course either of their lives took in the future, they'd be best friends until their dying days. Jo was certain of that.

Boyfriends came and went, as did other friends. Even Jo's parents were no longer around. They weren't dead. Although they may as well have been. Jo hardly ever saw them. That was a decision that worked well for all parties concerned. The greater the distance between Jo, her mum and her dad, the happier they all were. Not that her mum and dad ever seemed happy. They were miserable when they were married and they were miserable apart. Basically, they were miserable people. They were only ever happy if they were moaning about something or arguing with someone. Jo had left home the minute she could; her dad had left just one week later. Although he'd left before and come back. So many times, in fact, that some of the neighbours started calling him Yoyo.

Jo left to go and stay at Neva's. It had been a second home to Jo nearly all her life. Then she and Neva had moved to London together and bought their flat.

Yep. Being Neva's best friend was definitely the best thing to happen to her.

She smiled at the thought. She had said as much to Neva more than once and Neva, ever the optimist, had replied, 'The best thing … so far. Better things than me lay ahead, Jo. I'm sure of it.' But then Neva had always been a bit of a nutter. She genuinely believed in happy endings.

Mind you, perhaps Neva had a point. She was now with Rafe. And he was one hell of a happy ending. It was early days though. Neva and Rafe had only been dating since Christmas Eve. Anything could go wrong.

'Damn it!' Jo chastised herself. She really must try to stop looking on the downside of love. Just because her parents' marriage had been like a warzone, and just because she seemed incapable of settling down herself, that didn't mean Neva wouldn't get her fairy-tale ending.

Jo wouldn't mind a fairy-tale ending with Gavin. He was hot. He was fit. He lived and worked at Wynter House, which meant that if he married, his wife would probably live there too. Jo could handle being the wife of the estate manager cum groundskeeper cum handyman of a stately home. But she didn't want to get married. And Gavin was playing hard to get. So no fairy-tale ending in sight.

What on earth was wrong with her? She loved her new job. She loved the flat. She loved her new life. She was just feeling a bit down for some reason.

Since Rafe had met his sister, Cat and her daughter, Kyra at the salon on Wednesday,

Neva had been spending most of her time at Wynter House. Neva had invited Jo to join them, so that she wouldn't be alone at the flat, but Jo had said she was fine.

Neva had popped back to Merriment Bay and the salon for a few hours on Thursday, and again on Friday afternoon, when she'd told Jo all about a body that might be lying beneath the floor of a hidden cellar in Devon Villa. Jo had thought she was making it up but Neva assured her it was true and told her that Cat had called Rafe and Adam that morning and they, in turn, had told Olivia. Jo could imagine how that had gone down, especially when Neva said that there had been a confession stating that a member of the Devon family was a murderer.

'A murderer?' Jo repeated, keen to hear more about it. 'One of the Devons? How did Cat, Kyra and Mary take that? But more to the point, how did Olivia take it? She hasn't had another heart attack, has she?"

'No. Thank God. But I think Rafe thought she might. He said everyone is in a state of shock – and he's right. Including me. I wanted to find out how Olivia reacted, which is why I stayed for lunch. Well, and to show my love and support for Rafe, of course.'

'Of course. Forget that. Tell me what Olivia said.'

'She didn't believe it at first. Like the rest of us. But when she realised he was serious, she was rather upset, according to Rafe. Which basically means she blew her top. Only he's far too polite and reserved to say that. She was horrified that it might make the news. She said it's bad enough that Rafe and Adam have accepted Cat and Kyra into the family. Now they have to contend with having the word 'murder' linked to the Wynter name. I don't know why she makes such a fuss about it. It's not as if the Wynters are in line to the throne or anything. Most people haven't even heard of them.'

'Delusions of grandeur. That's her problem.'

'Yeah. But I think, when she was young and first married to Sebastian, they were a fairly important family. At least in this county. I remember Ethel and Queenie telling me about the balls they held at Wynter House. Olivia is still living in the past. That's her real problem. Anyway, Rafe said he had to remain calm even though Olivia made some very unpleasant remarks. And I bet one or two of those were about me. That's all he said really. You know Rafe. Gossip isn't his thing. Neither is repeating entire conversations to his girlfriend, sadly. But he did say he told Olivia that Cat and everyone would be going to the house for Sunday lunch, including Mary Devon.'

'And she still didn't have another heart attack?'

'I know. It's unbelievable. He also said she wasn't best pleased to hear that Amias and Cat are dating. I don't think Cat and Kyra are going to get to meet Olivia for some time yet. But I could be wrong.'

Neva wasn't wrong, as she later told Jo when she phoned her after Sunday lunch. And she also said that Mary was thinking of selling Devon Villa and that there was a good chance Rowan and Nigel might be able to buy it. Neva had been more excited about that than anything else.

Perhaps that was why Jo was feeling a bit down today. Everything seemed to be going so well for Neva, which Jo was thrilled about. But sometimes lately, Jo did feel a bit envious. Just a little. She had never had a happy family, like Neva's. For a short time, she had spent some blissful summers at her granddad's, but he had died when she was quite young. She still had those happy memories but family life was something she associated more with arguments than with happiness.

Or perhaps it was simply because it was Monday. Jo had never liked Mondays. Although, since moving to Merriment Bay and effectively becoming her own boss, even though it was really Neva's business, Mondays had become much better.

She needed to shake off this melancholy mood. This wasn't like her at all.

Her phone beeped and she put her mug of coffee down as she reached for it. It was probably Neva texting to see if she was up. Neva would be surprised when Jo told her she'd been up since six and had been sitting by one of the French windows in their flat, looking out over the bay, and had watched the sun come up.

'Bloody hell!' Jo was the one who was surprised, so much so that she almost knocked her coffee over in astonishment.

It wasn't a text from Neva.

It was a text from Rob, Jo's ex-fiancé.

Chapter Four

'What do you think it means?' Jo held out her phone to Neva.

Neva tutted. She had just come from Wynter House and closed the door to their flat when Jo told her Rob had sent a text.

'Can I at least take off my coat? And maybe make a cup of coffee? I came as soon as I got your text so I haven't even had breakfast or anything.'

'I need to know how to respond.'

'That's hardly an emergency, is it?

'What made you think it was?'

'Your text. "Come quick. I need your help. This is an emergency." If it hadn't been for the "Love Jo" and all the emojis and kisses, I might have thought something dreadful had happened.'

Jo grinned. 'Oh yeah. Sorry. What can I tell you? It was early. I was in shock. And it sort of felt like an emergency at the time.'

'Really? That's the best you've got?' Neva

shook her head as she hung up her coat. 'I tried to call you. Why didn't you answer?'

'I was in the shower. I saw you'd called, but then I saw your text saying you were on your way, so I waited for you to get here.'

'You could've called me back. At least then I could've had some coffee before dashing down here. Now I've got to text Rafe and let him know everything's OK. Honestly, Jo. I'm the one who's usually the drama queen and in need of reassurance. Not you.'

'Yeah. Well. Our roles seem to have become reversed. It's Monday. You know I don't like Mondays. Just take a look at it will you, and tell me what you think?'

'I think I've been leaving you on your own too much. Why are you going so crazy over getting a text from Rob?'

Jo shrugged. 'I don't know. I truly don't. But the minute I saw it was from him – and what it said, I couldn't stop thinking about him. About us. About the fun we had. But mostly about the sex, if I'm honest. God. I *sooooo* miss having sex. I think that's what it is. Sex depravation. It's addled my brain.' She held out her phone again and this time Neva took it. Jo smiled. 'I'll make coffee. I'll even make some toast.'

Neva went into the sitting room and flopped onto an armchair.

'I'm just texting Rafe and then I'll look.'

She put Jo's phone beside her and sent a quick text telling Rafe there was nothing to worry about. It was just Jo being Jo. She grinned at the row of thumbs up, smiley faces and heart emojis he sent in reply. He'd only just started using emojis. Until recently his texts to her had just contained a couple of kisses at the end, but all Neva's had at least one row of emojis and he seemed to be getting the message. Neva liked emojis. He'd started off with one heart and now he was sending almost as many emojis as she was. But only to her. He told her, when she asked, that he never sent them to anyone else. And never, ever would. She was sure he'd almost sighed when he'd said that. As if he thought it was all a bit silly, but he was doing it because he loved her.

'Well?' Jo popped her head round the door.

'Sorry. Just about to look.' Neva put her phone down, picked up Jo's and read Rob's text out loud. "Hi, baby. I'm missing you already. I really want you back in my bed. I can't stop thinking about you and all the things we did. I need to see you again. The sooner the better. Call me, you sexy goddess." Bloody hell!'

'I know, right? Weird or what? It doesn't even sound like him.'

'Was he drunk when he sent it?'

'At 7.30 on a Monday morning? Yeah. That's likely.'

'OK. I was only asking because it's just so

weird. I mean, it is the sort of thing a drunk guy might text, isn't it?'

'I suppose so.' Jo disappeared back into the kitchen.

'Is this the first time you've heard from him since he threw you out?'

Neva glanced up from the screen but Jo didn't answer. She reappeared a few minutes later with a tray bearing a jug of orange juice, two glasses, two mugs, a pot of coffee, several slices of buttered toast and four croissants.

'Don't look at me like that. I'm stress-eating. What did you say? I didn't hear you.'

Neva repeated her question and Jo tutted loudly.

'He didn't throw me out. Exactly. OK, he sort of did. But I was going to leave anyway, don't forget. And yes. It's the first time since I moved down here.'

'Er. You don't think he could've sent this to you by mistake, do you?'

'What? You think he meant to send it to someone else? Is that what you're suggesting? That he's already having sex with someone new?'

Neva shrugged and handed Jo back her phone in exchange for the mug of coffee Jo gave her. Jo studied the screen again and slumped down onto the sofa.

'I don't know, Jo. But it would make more sense, in a way, than him sending you a text like that, completely out of the blue. I mean, if he was sending it to you, wouldn't he at least ask how you are? And whether you're enjoying your new life? And he ought to bloody well say how sorry he is for all those awful things he said to you.'

'You're right. And for that bloody list.'

'Oh yeah. The list. And talking of the list, would he really go from telling you all your so-called faults to telling you how much he's missing you and how great you are in bed?'

'I was pretty great in bed. So that part's understandable.' Jo grinned and winked at Neva. 'But I see your point. Although he is a man. And this is Rob we're talking about. He always did have a habit of only ever seeing things from his point of view. Maybe he's calmed down, realised he misses me and how brilliant I am and how wrong he was, but he can't bring himself to say that. So instead, he sends a text about how fantastic the sex was. He clearly knows me better than I thought.'

Neva laughed. 'Oh come on. Are you telling me that he's dumb enough to think that all he has to do is talk about great sex and you'll go running back to him? And let's not forget Christmas. And his mum. And that you said yourself you hadn't had sex since you moved in with him and it hadn't been great for a while.'

Jo eyed Neva over the rim of her mug. 'Hmmm. I'd almost forgotten about

Charmaine.' She shivered dramatically and grinned. 'And you're right. Things weren't that good at the end. But until we got engaged and then moved in together things had been fine. And frankly, even boring sex is better than no sex. Although as we haven't seen each other for three weeks or so, the sex might be great again. Like it was when we first starting dating. Perhaps I should text him back and see what happens. What do you think?'

'I think, unless you actually do miss him and want to see him again, you should send a text back along the lines of, "Did you send this to me by mistake?" and see how he replies to that.'

Jo looked thoughtful as she bit into a slice of toast. She grabbed a croissant with her other hand and swung her legs up onto the sofa so that she was stretched the full length of it, but still facing Neva in the armchair.

'Or ... I could send a text back saying if he's ever down this way he can give me a call. That way, I'm playing hard to get. And men like women who do that. And I'm not saying I miss him or anything. Or that I want him back. So if, by some chance, the git is seeing someone new and meant the text for her and not me, I won't look foolish, or desperate, or sad, or anything. What about that?'

'That's good. You see. You didn't need me at all. You had the answer all along. Which is why I always turned to you for advice about my love life in the past.' Neva picked up a croissant and took a bite. 'Although ... by saying he can call you, isn't that sort of saying you do miss him and you would be happy to see him again?'

'Damn it. I suppose that's true.' Jo reached out for another slice of toast even though she hadn't touched the croissant yet. 'The annoying thing is, I do miss him. A bit. Just a little. Sometimes. And I would quite like to see him again. Just once. Or twice. He was good looking, wasn't he? And we could have sex right away, whereas with anyone else, I've got to get to know them and go through all that dating stuff. I'm beginning to think Gavin really isn't interested in me, so he's probably a non-starter. Sometimes I just miss holding someone. You know? Just being in someone's arms.' She let out a long, melancholy sigh.

'I understand that completely. I miss Rafe on the few nights we don't sleep together. But do you really want to be back in Rob's arms, Jo? Do you want to go back to what you had? And more importantly, do you want to leave our business here in Merriment Bay and go back to Upminster to live? Because that's what would have to happen, wouldn't it? Eventually.'

Jo's mouth dropped open and she stared at Neva.

'I hadn't even considered that. You're right. There's no way I'm leaving here. Or you.

Or my new life. I'm going to delete that text right now. I'm not even going to reply.' She picked up her phone and her fingers hovered over the screen. 'But it doesn't have to get that far, does it? I mean, I could just see him once or twice every couple of weeks. Just for the night. We wouldn't have to actually get back together. Hmmm. Perhaps this needs a bit more thought.'

Neva shook her head and laughed. 'And you call me a nutter? But at least you may find out if the text was meant for you or not. If it was, you'll possibly hear from him again. If it wasn't, he still might text you to tell you it was sent to you by mistake and ask you to delete it.'

Chapter Five

Rafe knew it wouldn't take long for word to get out, both about the fact that Catherine Devon and her daughter, Kyra were Wynters, or about the body in the cellar at Devon Villa.

Rafe had told all the guests and staff at Wynter House about both. He was fairly certain none of them would gossip to anyone outside of the house ... apart from Cecil and Ronnie, but he wanted people to know that it was a member of the Wynter family who had made Cat and Kyra's relationship to the Wynters, public knowledge.

The best way to do that was to tell Bartholomew Raine, the vicar of St Mary-in-the-Fields, the bijou church in the centre of Merriment Bay, in the full knowledge that to do so would ensure all the residents of Merriment Bay would eventually hear it, either from Bartholomew, or more likely from his wife, Constance. And Monday morning was as good a time as any.

Rafe used the, admittedly feeble, excuse of taking the Reverend a bottle of Wyntersleap Gin. Bartholomew was clearly thrilled to think he was one of the first, outside of those at Wynter House and the village of Wyntersleap, to taste it and thanked Rafe profusely.

'This is so kind and thoughtful of you, Rafe. But then you're such a kind and thoughtful man. I've always said as much and so has my dear wife. Constance and I do like the occasional tipple of an evening, and gin is our poison of choice. Oh, not that I'm in any way suggesting your gin will taste like poison. It's merely a saying.'

Rafe stopped himself from laughing and simply smiled. 'Yes. I've heard the saying. I hope you'll both enjoy the gin. We'll be selling it via a website and also at the Wyntersleap Inn when the pub's back up and running. Sean Small is a partner in the Wyntersleap distillery. We'll be giving generous discounts to our 'friends' on all purchases. And speaking of friends, you and your wife are friends with Mary Devon, aren't you?'

Bartholomew tensed a little. 'We are.'

'Then I have news I'd like to share with you.'

Bartholomew leant forward conspiratorially. 'Is it about the body in the cellar? I must confess I already know. My dear wife and I, along with our nephew, Francis were having dinner at Devon Villa on the night in question. In fact, Mary wanted Francis' expert opinion on a painting they'd discovered. He's an art conservator. I'm sure I must have mentioned that many times. Although we don't see much of you and your family. Very little in fact. But you have the estate to run, I know. Francis was the one who found the confession. Oh, unless it isn't about that, in which case I suppose I should explain.'

'No need. I'm aware of the body and the confession, although I wasn't aware it was your nephew who found it, so I would like to hear more on that.'

'Then do sit down and we'll have coffee and biscuits and I'll tell you all about it. Oh, but you had news you wanted to tell me. I do veer off the track sometimes. Please take a seat.'

By the time Rafe had broken his news to Bartholomew and the Reverend had filled Rafe in about Francis, almost an hour had passed. Having drunk two cups of coffee, and refused a Bourbon biscuit several times, Rafe made his excuses and finally got away.

He decided to call into The Mane Event and see how Neva and Jo were getting on with their redecorating. It seemed to be taking them an inordinate amount of time to paint a few walls, especially as Neva's dad Dennis was helping from time to time. But that was possibly because both Neva and Jo kept changing their minds about the exact shade of blue they wanted. Most people decided after painting a test area; Neva and Jo appeared unable to decide until they had painted the entire salon. And then they repainted it another shade of blue.

'I merely gave Reverend Raine the facts,' Rafe told Neva when she asked how he had got on. 'And a bottle of Wyntersleap Gin. I said that my father, Phillip and Cat's mother, Mary had been lovers and had had a child together. A child whom, it had been decided at the time, for better or worse, was to be kept a secret. The Reverend was already aware of the body in the cellar, having been at Devon Villa on the evening of the discovery of the confession, so he could fill me in on some of the details Cat left out. Like the fact that his nephew, Francis is helping him write the history of the Raine family and that Jerusalem, whose body it's believed to be, is Francis' pet project.'

'Really? Wow.'

'I just missed Francis. He's been here all weekend but returned to London this morning. He's an art conservator. Freelance apparently. And the best in the country, according to Constance Raine. Oh. Don't mention the bit about Francis writing the family history, to Olivia. This might not die a death as soon as I'd hoped if Francis Raine writes about it. Apparently, he's intent on digging up everything he can. Excuse the pun. Not the body, of course. That's being done by experts, as we speak.'

'As Olivia avoids me at all costs, I don't think you need to worry about me telling her anything. Did the Reverend say anything else? Was he shocked about your dad and Mary?'

'Utterly. He thought Alwick Wells was Cat's dad. Somewhat annoyingly, he assured me he'd keep the news to himself. Not that I really believe that for one minute. But I informed him there was no need to keep it a secret. We were all more than happy for the relationship to be made public. Not that it is really anyone's business. I think the news should reach every house in the village by this weekend, if not sooner.'

'Remind me never to tell the Reverend anything,' Jo said, peeling the lid off a tin of blue paint and pouring it into two trays.

'And me,' added Neva, dipping her paint roller in one of them.

This blue was a slightly lighter shade than the one on the seemingly finished walls, so it looked as if they had changed their minds again. Rafe chose not to comment. Just in case. He, Adam and Gavin had offered, more than once, to help, but Neva and Jo said they could manage perfectly well. From the amount of paint each of them had on their clothes, Rafe wasn't sure that was true. But he decided it was best not to comment on that either.

'I lied a little.' Rafe stepped back a few inches as he eyed the paint-laden roller in Neva's hand. 'I said that once Olivia was aware that Catherine and Kyra Devon were now living in Merriment Bay and that Viola Devon had passed away, she had revealed the secret to me and Adam, deciding it had been kept from us for far too long. I added that we'd all immediately agreed to welcome our relatives into the fold.'

'Really? You lied to a vicar?'

Neva wagged her finger at him, obviously forgetting she was holding the paint roller, and Rafe had to jump out of the way of the arc of blue paint she sent flying in his direction. Luckily, only a few spots landed on him. And they were in his hair and on his face. Jo threw him a cloth as she laughed at him.

'That's what comes from lying to a man of God,' she quipped.

Neva laughed, but she did apologise as she placed the paint roller in its tray.

'Does Olivia know she's welcomed her relatives into the fold? Or haven't you broken that to her yet?'

Rafe grinned and having cleaned off the paint, tossed the cloth back to Jo who caught it in one hand.

'She knows. I told her this morning shortly after you left. She wasn't pleased but in the end

43

she agreed that it must seem as if the family are united in this matter. Although she did add, that whilst she has breath in her body, she will never accept "those women" as her kin.' The grin faded from his face. 'I thought, after nearly losing Adam, and her own heart attack, she might have mellowed just a tad. But now with this business of the body in the cellar, she seems determined not to be swayed. She was even more stubborn on that point this morning than she was on Friday or on Sunday.'

'She'll come round, Rafe. Eventually. I don't really know her, of course, and you've known her all your life, but for someone who holds such store by family, she must be curious to see her son's daughter, surely? And to have a great-granddaughter must mean something to her.'

'That's what I was hoping. But she doesn't appear to be in the least bit interested to meet them. Ever.'

'Just ignore her,' Jo said. 'I realise she's your grandmother and all that but she strikes me as a bit of a bully. She likes to intimidate people and she expects them to do her bidding. But I bet she won't like being left out. If you just carry on regardless, as if it doesn't matter to any of you what she thinks or whether she ever meets Cat and Kyra, nothing will annoy her more. Tell her she can remain in her rooms if she wants to, but tell her all the lovely things you're going to be doing with Cat and Kyra. She'll soon want to be involved.'

Rafe frowned. 'It's worth a try. She does like to feel she's the head of the family. The matriarch. Being ignored might make her think things through. At the moment, I tell her everything.' He grinned at Neva. 'Well, not quite everything. But everything pertaining to the house.'

'You didn't tell her about the distillery,' Neva pointed out.

'True. But that was for a good reason. I didn't want to open old wounds or for her to be disappointed if it didn't work. And come to think of it, Jo's right. She was more annoyed about being kept in the dark over that than she was about me going against her wishes. It was as if she would have wanted to be involved in all the trials and errors of Sean and me setting it up and perfecting the recipe.'

'Then perhaps we should start arranging some fun things at Wynter House,' Neva said. 'And not invite her to them. But make sure Judith tells her that they're going on.'

Rafe grinned. 'Perhaps we should.'

'And speaking of fun things.' Neva sidled up close. But not too close, as Rafe pointed at the paint down the front of her jumper. 'We haven't discussed what we're doing for Valentine's Day. It's just over a week away. You haven't changed your mind about it again, have

45

you?'

Rafe raised his brows. 'Again? Oh. You mean because Amelia had arranged for our Wyntersleep Gin launch to be on that day, before Sean, Adam and I decided to go a different path from the one she'd planned. No. I haven't changed my mind. You and I will do something special.'

'Isn't there a dance here on Valentine's Day?' Jo asked. 'Aren't you going to that?'

'Yes. It's the Merriment Bay Moonlight Valentine's Dance,' Rafe said.

Neva nodded. 'I told you, Jo. We're all going to that.' She smiled at Rafe. 'So whatever you and I are doing, it'll be during the day, won't it?'

'It will. And I have a plan.'

Neva tilted her head, seductively. 'What sort of plan?'

Rafe grinned and leant forward to kiss her on the lips, being careful that his coat didn't touch her jumper.

'That's for me to know and for you to find out. Now I'd better go. Sean, Adam and I are supposed to be batching up several hundred bottles of our gin this week.'

Chapter Six

Neva and Jo were finally happy with the shade of blue they had painted the walls of The Mane Event. It was called First Dawn and Neva told Rafe that the name of it had helped to sway them. He had shaken his head as if found their reasoning hard to comprehend, but he smiled, kissed her and said he was thrilled that at least she could tick off another thing on her ever-growing list of jobs to do before she and Jo could re-open the salon.

Cat and Kyra arrived at the salon on Wednesday to start working on the trompe l'oeil. On Monday, Neva had shown them the books she had borrowed from Rafe's library and they had taken them away to do some initial sketches.

Neva was particularly pleased when they both said the blue on the walls was the perfect complement to the colours they had in mind for the trompe l'oeil.

Rafe did, rather foolishly, comment on

that when Neva called to tell him.

'That's excellent news. But as it's an image of the goddess Venus rising out of the waves, with an expanse of sky behind her, wouldn't any shade of blue complement the sea and sky?'

Neva tutted. 'Philistine. I won't repeat that to your sister and niece. I thought posh people knew about the importance of stuff like that.'

'By "stuff like that" do you mean the subtleties and nuances of ...? No.' He laughed jovially. 'I'm not even going to pretend I know anything about art. And I'd hardly categorise myself as posh. But I do like hearing the words sister and niece. I'm quickly growing accustomed to the fact that I'm Cat's brother and Kyra's uncle. Although I'm not sure I'm any good at being either, yet.'

Neva laughed too. 'Well, you *are* posh. And still rather prim and proper at times. Although my influence is definitely having a detrimental effect on that. And you're a brilliant brother to Cat and uncle to Kyra. They both said, only a matter of minutes ago, how wonderful you and Adam have been and how much they love having you both in their lives. Oh, and for your information, "stuff like that" is a technical term.'

Rafe laughed louder. 'Of course it is. And *for your information,* nothing you do could ever have a detrimental effect on me, only a positive one. I thought I was happy until I met you. Now I realise I was merely passing time. I love having Cat and Kyra in my life, but without you, Neva Grey, I'd still be that somewhat cold-hearted, morose and taciturn man you met before Christmas. I love you, Neva.'

A warm glow flushed over Neva. 'I love you too. I wish you were here so I could show you how much. Or I was there with you. But I'll have to wait until tonight, because Cat and Kyra are going to be working on the trompe l'oeil today, and Jo and I still have a million and one things to do before we can think of re-opening. Which reminds me. Have you fixed a new date for the official launch of Wyntersleap Gin? Only Jo and I would like to have a bit of a do here for our re-opening, and obviously, we don't want our dates to clash.'

'Sorry. What was that? I was thinking about tonight.' He cleared his throat and laughed. 'Seriously though. Sean, Adam and I are leaning towards the end of February.'

'We're considering the week after Valentine's Day, so that would be OK, wouldn't it? We're just going to have cocktails and nibbles. That's canapés to posh people. Probably with a beach theme. Have you decided what you're doing?'

'I like the sound of nibbles. No. We haven't decided. I don't regret letting Amelia go, but the three of us are stumped for ideas. We're still considering inviting some press and potential buyers. We'll serve them lunch, get them to try the gin and then bring them to the house, via Wyntersleap Falls for afternoon tea, followed by a tour of the distillery. Then return to the house for cocktails ... and possibly 'nibbles'. But if you've got any ideas, or if Jo has, I'd love to hear them.'

'We'll have a think and let you know. Perhaps you could ask Cat and Kyra. It might be nice to get them involved. Not that I'm trying to tell you how to run your life or your business.'

'That's a fantastic idea. I don't know why it hadn't occurred to me. You're a genius.'

'And you thought I was just a pretty face.'

'Oh no I didn't. I knew the minute I saw you that you were so much more than that. Which brings me nicely on to the next thing I wanted to run by you. The village isn't looking too bad now the flood waters have receded but there's a visible tidemark on most of the cottages. We need to get those painted. Strictly speaking, we're only responsible for the ones we own, but Adam and I have discussed it and we feel we want to cover the cost of painting all of them. Outside at least. I was going to have a word with your dad and Nigel. Do you think they might be interested in taking on the job?'

'Interested? I'm sure they'd be happy to do it. And they'd give you a much better price than anyone else. That's because you're dating me, in case you had any doubt.'

'No doubt at all. That was one of the reasons I want them.' Rafe laughed down the phone. 'But not the only one. I know they'll do an excellent job, based on the work they did here over Christmas. We're starting to make money from our gin but it'll be a while until we see much real profit, so any discount at all will be greatly appreciated, but I don't expect them to work at a loss. They're in business too and need to make a profit. And of course, we can include as much gin as your dad and Nigel want, in with the payment.'

'I'm pretty sure they'll do it for cost, so the gin will be a bonus. Although Rowan may try to insist on getting a little something extra out of it. Like you letting Sasha come and stay at Wynter House for a weekend or two. My sister knows how to drive a hard bargain.'

'Sasha's welcome to stay whenever she wants. Although, perhaps I'd better check with Archie. No. You know I'm joking. Archie adores her and her practical jokes. I'll give your dad and Nigel a call this afternoon. Now I suppose I'd better get back to the gin. Who knew owning a distillery involved so much work?'

Chapter Seven

Now that the walls of the salon had been painted and Cat and Kyra were working on the trompe l'oeil, there wasn't much Neva and Jo could do in the salon without either getting in Cat and Kyra's way moving things around, or creating dust by drilling holes for the hooks on which the mirrors, racks for the hairdryers and other styling tools, would hang. So instead, they decided to redecorate the flat.

They had done a few bits here and there prior to moving in, but painting the salon walls had made them realise the flat could do with a bit of brightening up.

'What about using the same blue paint we used downstairs?' Neva suggested.

'Or yellow,' Jo countered.

'Why yellow? Not that I'm against the idea but with all the windows letting in so much light, perhaps a cooler colour might be better.'

'I thought we were brightening the place up?'

'We are. But there's brightening up and there's burning holes in your eyes. Yellow might come under the latter.'

'I wasn't suggesting bright yellow, like the sun. I was thinking more of a soft buttery hue. Or maybe white with a hint of yellow. Rob painted the living room in our house a buttercup yellow and it was really warm and welcoming. The paint colour, not the house. Although that was warm and welcoming at first. Before Charmaine came to stay.'

Neva threw her a questioning look. 'Have you heard from him since that text on Monday?'

Jo gave a small cough. 'No.'

'Does no mean yes and you don't want to tell me?'

Jo tutted. 'No. You know I always tell you everything.' She got up and headed towards the kitchen. 'Although ... I think I may have forgotten to mention that I did send him a text this morning.' She stopped at the door and turned back to look at Neva. 'Just a short one. And only because I hadn't heard from him since Monday and as it's Thursday today, it didn't look as if I'd hear from him again unless I replied to his text.'

'Jo!' Neva sighed and shook her head. 'Do you want to hear from him?'

'Oh, I don't know. Until I got that text, I'd only thought about him a couple of times. And that was just because after four years together and an engagement, you don't simply forget someone just like that, do you? But I kept looking at that text and wondering about what you said. That it might not have been meant for me. I just want to know either way. Don't ask me why but I do.'

'What did you say in your text? And more importantly, has he replied?'

Jo let out a sigh. 'I'll make some coffee and then I'll tell you.'

'Jo? Tell me now and then make the coffee.'

'Oh OK. I said that I was surprised to get his text. That I'm loving life here. That I hoped he was happy and that if he was down this way at any time in the near future, he could give me a call. I sent it at 8 and he hasn't replied. But I didn't reply to his text for four days, so I can't expect an immediate response, can I?'

'But you do, don't you?'

Jo let out another sigh. Longer this time. 'Yeah. I do. I thought about everything you said and I'm sure I don't want him back. Not really. But the thing is, we have history. I miss having a boyfriend. Someone I can send silly texts to like you do to Rafe. Someone to call me and tell me they love me. And obviously, I miss the sex. That goes without saying. Rob and I could fall back into our relationship so easily. OK, we did say a few nasty things to one another, and his mum drives me insane. I definitely don't want to move back to Upminster. But being with him was nice. Most of the time. It was safe. I was happy. I miss it. I miss him.'

'Oh, Jo. I'm sorry. But I thought you were lusting after Gavin?'

'I was. I am. But he's not lusting after me, that much seems clear.'

'You've hardly spent any time at Wynter House for the last week or so. He might be lusting after you now. They say absence makes the heart grow fonder. And it clearly does if you're thinking of getting back with Rob.'

'I know. It's crazy, isn't it? But sometimes the past has a hold on us and we don't even realise it until something like a bloody silly text pings on our phone and makes us miss someone we thought we were well and truly over.'

'What are you going to do?'

Jo shrugged. 'Until I hear from Rob, there's not really anything I can do, is there? Apart from paint this sitting room a lovely, calming, warm and welcoming shade of yellow.' She fluttered her eyelashes and clasped her hands together in a pleading gesture.

Neva laughed and threw a cushion at her.

'OK. We'll paint the sitting room yellow.'

Chapter Eight

'Today is going to be one of those days, I think,' Neva said to Jo when she phoned her around 9 on Friday morning. 'It began badly when Cat phoned Rafe to say the press had contacted her at Amias' house. They'd tracked down Mary, who's now staying there and wanted to interview not just her but also Cat and Kyra. Amias told her to say no and that they had no comment on the matter. But Cat told Rafe that the phone has been ringing off its hook and Amias is now answering all her calls unless he recognises the number.'

'Can't she just tell them to bugger off? That's what I would do.'

'That's sort of what Rafe did. About ten minutes after Cat had called, he got a phone call too. Only they asked him about his dad's affair, why Cat had been kept a secret, when did he find out, and what did he feel about the Wynters having a killer in the family. Needless to say, he wasn't pleased. Especially when the regional media started calling as well as the local press. He gave them a brief statement basically saying that he and Adam, along with Cat had no knowledge of her parentage until recently, due to a decision made by his late father. Rafe told me it's always preferable to blame the dead. He said that his sister and her daughter were immediately welcomed at Wynter House as soon as all parties became aware of the relationship. Or something like that. I can't recall the exact words. He added that it was a private, family matter and asked them to respect the privacy of everyone concerned.'

'Which they won't.'

'That's exactly what Rafe said. He's asked me to let him know if anyone contacts me, or you, or my family, but I'm not sure they will. If anyone contacts you though, you won't say anything, will you?'

'Other than to tell them to go and drown themselves? No. My lips are sealed. Even if they offer me millions for my story about the love and lust and scandalous lives of the Wynters and the Devons and the Greys.' Jo laughed down the phone.

'Rafe said they'll probably run around asking questions and trying to dig up dirt. Both regarding Jerusalem Raine and everyone involved in her murder, or related to anyone who was, and also regarding him and his new-found family. But eventually they'll get bored and go away. As he says, it's not really anyone else's business, is it? And he, unlike Olivia, doesn't think anyone, other than those who know the Wynters and the Devons, will be in the least bit interested. OK, a body in a cellar is fairly interesting but once the coroner gives his verdict and makes his report, and everyone realises this all happened hundreds of years ago, they'll soon forget about it.'

'Yeah. The Wynters aren't aristocracy. Or famous. Even if Olivia likes to think they are.'

'One good thing has come of it. Wyntersleap Gin is getting a lot of good reviews. That's not because of this, but it's nice to know. But Judith told Rafe that visitor ticket sales for the Wynter House tours have shot through the roof in just a matter of hours, and that there's also been a phenomenal amount of new interest in the Wyntersleap Gin Tours. We don't know if it's because of the long-lost sibling bit, or because the long-lost sibling also appears to be descended from a thief and a murderer, or just because people have heard about the gin and want to come and see where it's made. We're all hoping it's that last part.'

'The gin's delicious, so I expect it is.'

'Would you mind if I spend today here with him? You're welcome to come and join us. It's just that I want to be with him to give him my support. He doesn't need it, but I want to do it anyway.'

'Of course I don't mind. I won't join you though. Will you be here tomorrow? Or are you going to spend the weekend at Wynter House? It's OK if you want to. I don't mind at all. There's plenty I can be getting on with.'

'I would quite like to, if you're sure. But why don't you come too? If not today, then tomorrow. Gavin actually asked after you last night. He said he hadn't seen you for a while and neither has George. He said he misses you.'

'Gavin misses me? Wow! Things are looking up.'

'Oh no. Sorry. I meant George said he misses you. Gavin did ask after you though and said the bit about not seeing you for a while.'

'But it was George who's missing me?'

'Yes. Gavin might be too. He just didn't want to say so.'

'Yeah right. And that was a pig flying past the window.'

'Come here for the weekend. I'm not taking no for an answer. Let's see if we can do something wild and crazy and upset Olivia.'

'Now there's an offer I can't refuse.'

Chapter Nine

Neva called Jo again just before 5 that evening.

'Why don't you come and join us tonight?'

Having spent most of the day alone, repainting her bedroom a soft shade of lavender, Jo was tempted, but she hadn't washed her hair that morning and she had somehow managed to get covered in paint from head to toe. Plus she'd spilt some on the floor. She'd have to clean all that up before having a shower and doing her hair and by the time she'd done all that, it would be a mad rush to get to Wynter House in time for dinner, let alone drinks beforehand. And Jo could do with a drink. She also needed something to eat before 8 p.m. She hadn't eaten all day and she just realised she was starving.

'Nah. But thanks. I'll see you sometime tomorrow and you can update me on everything.'

'But it's Friday night.'

'So? I have been alone on a Friday night

before, you know. I think I can handle it. In fact, it'll be nice to have the place to myself. I can have a long, relaxing bath and wander around naked without fear of Rafe turning up. Sorry. That didn't come out quite the way it sounded in my head. I wasn't moaning.'

Neva laughed. 'What is wrong with you? As if I'd take offence at anything you said. We've been best friends for far too long. But please don't say you want to be alone unless you really mean it. Don't say that for my sake. I can come back this evening if you want and then return here later, for the night.'

'That's just silly. No. You stay there. I'll be there in the morning. I'm fine. Honestly. And I want an early night. I've been painting my bedroom all day and I'm shattered.'

'OK. If you're sure. But if you change your mind just call and let me know. I'm happy to come back for the evening, honestly.'

'You're a nutter. I've said that before and I'll say it again. But I'm glad you are. Don't come back. I'll be fine. And I expect Rafe needs you right now. I know he said he's not bothered about all the gossip and the press but it must be a bit upsetting to have your private life plastered across the paper, even if it is just read by about ten people.'

'I know. I'm sure Rafe can handle it. And so can Adam, I think. But Olivia's already had one heart attack. I'm sure Rafe's wondering if all this will cause another. Although when he told her that they'd met Cat and Kyra on Wednesday, she took that news without keeling over. He said she seemed to be more annoyed that it had happened in our salon than the fact that it had happened at all. And when he told her about the body, she was fine. Well, not fine. She went mad. But what I meant was her heart was fine.'

'I know what you meant. I can see why he's worried. And that's why he needs you there to kiss his worries away, or some such crap. Now get lost because I seem to have got a bit of paint on my clothes and I need to get it out while I can. I'll see you in the morning.'

'A bit of paint? Jo? Is there anything you want to tell me?'

Jo studied the pool of blue paint on the wooden floor.

'Nope. Nothing at all. Bye for now.'

Jo quickly rang off and spent the next hour or so trying to remove the paint. Which proved to be a lot more difficult than she expected. By the time she had finished, it was almost 6.15 and she was ravenous. Either several lorries were rumbling along Coast Road, or it was her stomach growling with hunger.

She glanced out of the window and saw a man across the road holding a large, white paper bag with the logo 'The Perfect Plaice'. That was the fish and chip shop, a few doors away. She would have to cross a couple of roads to get there but she could be there and back in a matter of minutes. Could she go out looking like this? She glanced down at her paint-splattered jeans and jumper.

Sod it. There was hardly anyone about. She might look a complete and utter mess but no one important would see her. Gavin would be working in the gardens at Wynter House, or getting ready for drinks by now. There was no one else in Merriment Bay she needed to impress. And she was so hungry she could eat a shark. She grabbed her bag and ran downstairs.

The smell of battered fish and freshly fried chips wafted towards her even before she reached the door which she shoved open without looking.

'Jesus Christ! Are you trying to knock me out?' a deep voice yelled.

'Sorry. I wasn't looking.' Jo smiled apologetically at the man whose nose she might have just broken, if the dripping blood was anything to go by. 'Does it hurt?'

'Not at all.' His dark brown eyes glared at her. 'Of course it bloody hurts. You just shoved a solid glass door in my face.'

'I didn't do it on purpose. You shouldn't have been standing right behind it.'

'I was putting up a sign.'

'A sign? On the door?'

'Yes. What's wrong with putting a sign on the door?'

Jo shrugged. 'It's a glass door.'

'No. Really?'

Jo sighed. 'Glass is for looking through. Not for sticking signs on.'

'What are you? The decoration police?'

'No. But I do have an eye for design and glass doors shouldn't have signs stuck to them. You're dripping blood on the floor. You might want to tip your head back and maybe, get a hanky or something.' She glanced around. 'Where's the owner?'

'You're looking at him.'

'You're not the owner.' She rummaged in her bag and pulled out a packet of tissues. 'He's short and fat and cheerful. He looks a bit like Father Christmas. Or maybe that should be Friar Tuck. Get it? *Fryer* Tuck.'

'Don't give up the day job. And thanks for the compliments about my dad. I'm sure he'll give you extra batter for those kind remarks.'

Jo swallowed a tiny lump in her throat. 'Your dad? I meant those comments in a good way.'

'I'm sure you did. Ouch!'

He pushed Jo's hand aside as she tried to catch the blood, and instead, he caught her eye with his elbow.

'Owwww!' Jo shrieked. 'There was no need for that.'

'God. I'm sorry. I didn't do it on purpose.' He leant forward to take a closer look and dripped blood down her paint-splattered jumper.'

'Great. Now you're covering me in blood. Thanks a lot.'

'You can't even see it amongst all that paint. If that outfit's your idea of design, I'm not sure you should be giving advice about sticking signs on glass doors. Seriously. Are you OK?'

'I'll live.'

She held another tissue over her weeping eye, as her stomach groaned so loudly that both she and the man looked down at it.

'That sounded like something out of a horror movie. Are you carrying an alien or something in there?'

'How dare you be so rude about my beautiful baby!'

'Baby?' He looked genuinely shocked. 'You're pregnant? Bloody hell. I apologise. I was only joking. You don't look pregnant. You look fantastic. Shit. No. What I meant was you don't look fat. I mean. You don't look as if you're expecting. Why are you grinning?'

'I was winding you up. I'm not pregnant. I'm just starving.'

'Oh.' His cheeks had a reddish hue and a slow smile appeared on his full mouth as tiny lines formed around his brown, chocolate-drop eyes. 'So you came in for fish and chips then? Not to disfigure me, insult my dad and berate my design skills?'

'Yes. And I could eat a shark.'

'OK. Shark and chips coming up. Just as soon as I do something about my broken nose.'

'Oh God. Is it really broken? I'm so sorry.'

He grinned. 'Nope. I was winding you up.'

She grinned back as he walked around the counter and disappeared for a moment, returning with a wet cloth, folded into a thin line and draped across his nose. He leant back against the worktop behind him, laden with metal tubs and plastic containers and piles of paper and paper bags.

'Er. I don't really want shark. Not that you've got it, obviously.'

'I've got monkfish. Some people call that angelshark. Not that it tastes anything like shark.'

'How do you know that?'

'Because I've eaten shark in Japan.'

'You've been to Japan?'

He grinned again. 'That's not the usual reaction I get to that statement. Most people are surprised I've eaten shark, not that I've been to Japan. Although several places in the UK sell shark these days, so lots of people have tried it.' The grin faded slightly. 'Or were you surprised that the son of a short, fat fish-fryer could afford to go to Japan?'

'No. And I really wasn't criticising your dad. Although I can see that you might take it that way. I was surprised because Japan is a place I've always wanted to visit. At cherry blossom time.'

'That's when I was there. It's breathtakingly beautiful.'

'Did you see lots of koi carp?'

He gave her an odd look over the wet cloth. 'Yes, I did.'

Jo let out a sigh. 'I love koi carp. They remind me of my granddad. He had a pond full of koi and I could hand feed them.' She closed her eyes and let her mind wander. 'I can still feel their lips sucking the fish food from my fingers. They felt like a rubber band tightening on my skin. It tickled. God. I loved those summers at his house. Just me and Gramps sitting in the garden watching the fish for hours and hours, away from my mum and dad yelling and throwing things at one another.' Her stomach grumbled again and her eyes shot open. 'Sorry! I have no idea why I just told you all that.'

'It sounded nice.' He smiled and pushed himself away from the worktop, removing the cloth and glancing in the fish-shaped mirror opposite. 'I think it's stopped bleeding. And I think we'd better get you fed. Would you like to try the monkfish?'

Jo blushed as she shook her head. 'No.

Rock and chips please.'

He grinned. 'We call it Huss down here. One shark-sized Huss coming right up. Are you going to take it away or eat it here?'

She hesitated for a moment. Talking to this man had cheered her up, even if her eye was hurting like hell. She was tempted to stay and see if they could continue their conversation, but then she caught a glimpse of herself in the fish-shaped mirror and gasped. She looked an utter mess. Not only was there paint on her clothes, she had paint in her hair and on her face, and her hair, which she had tied loosely with an old scrunchy, had worked its way loose in places and was sticking out at odd angles. She wore no make-up and her eye was slowly swelling and the eyelid closing. She had to get out of there as fast as she could.

'Take away, please.' She hung her head and studied the floor.

'It's genuine vinyl,' he said. 'You're clearly wondering because you're staring at it.'

She glanced up and wished she hadn't. A look of horror swept across his face.

'Dear God! Did I do that? Of course I did.' He hurried around the counter and came and took her hands in his and led her towards a table, kicking out a chair with his foot. 'Sit down. I'll get you a wet cloth.'

'There's no need.'

He had already disappeared, but he was

back in a couple of seconds and leant forward to dab at her eye.

She leant back and edged away, peering at the cloth.

'It's not the one I used for my nose.' He could clearly read her mind. 'It's a clean one. Let me do this. It'll help, I promise.'

A man was singing in the background and she heard the voice of the short, fat man she had thought was the owner.

'What's been going on here then, Ed? Is that blood on the floor?'

'Yes Dad. We've had a bit of an accident.'

'An accident? Here? Was it our fault?'

'Yes and no.'

Jo shook her head as best she could. 'It was my fault. I shoved the door open and broke your son's nose and he accidently elbowed me in the eye.'

'Do what? How did that happen?'

'It doesn't matter. It's all fine. I hope.' Ed gave Jo a winning smile.

She smiled back, even though it hurt her eye to do so. 'It's all fine.'

'Shall I make you a nice cup of tea, young lady?' The father peered around his son.

'That's a good idea, Dad.' The man nodded to his left. 'This is my dad, Victor. And I'm Ed. Ed Fisher.'

'Fisher?' Jo couldn't help but grin.

'I know, right? But it could've been worse.

My surname could've been Fryer.'

'I'm Jo. Jo Duncan. I'm pleased to meet you both. Although I'd have preferred not to have been looking like this.'

'I'm pleased to meet you, Jo. And there's nothing at all wrong with the way you look. I'd have preferred not to have a broken nose.'

'Is it really broken?' She took the cloth from him and dabbed at her eye as he moved away a fraction.

'I doubt it. Even if it is, it won't be the first time. I used to play rugby. I've broken a lot more than my nose over the years.'

Victor Fisher brought the tea and bent down to retrieve a piece of bloodstained paper from the floor.

'Oh. Was that your sign?' Jo asked. 'What was it for?'

Ed nodded. 'The Merriment Bay Moonlight Valentine's Dance. Do you live around here? You've obviously been here before because you remembered my dad.'

'I've just moved down here. I live with my best friend, Neva above the salon, The Mane Event. Neva owns the place. Well, her mum and dad do really but that's not important. I'm running the business with her and sharing her flat.'

'I heard someone had bought the place,' Ed said. 'I know where to go for a haircut now.'

'We're not open yet. We were planning to

open around Valentine's Day but we're delaying for another week or so. We want to get the place perfect before we open.'

'This is The Perfect Plaice,' Victor said, laughing and pointing to the logo above the fish-shaped mirror before disappearing into the back.

Jo's stomach grumbled and this time it didn't seem to want to stop.

'I'll get you your food,' Ed said, laughing, as the front door opened.

A blonde, buxom woman tottered towards Ed on heels far too high which clearly impeded her ability to walk properly.

'What the hell happened to your nose, baby?'

Her high-pitched voice made Jo cringe, and Ed flushed crimson as the woman kissed him on the cheek.

'Er. I had an accident. It's nothing. Let me serve this lady her food. She's been waiting far too long already.'

He hurried behind the counter and the blonde woman looked Jo up and down.

'You look like you've been in the wars, love.'

Jo nodded as the woman glanced from her to Ed and back again. She was far too young to be Ed's mum but she definitely looked older than Ed, by at least ten years. Yet she had called him baby. Perhaps Ed liked older women. She gave Jo one final look before shrugging and disappearing out of sight, the same way Victor had. Jo was about to ask who she was when the woman reappeared wearing an apron stretched tight across her chest.

Victor was singing in the back room, Ed concentrated on frying and Jo drank her tea while the woman wiped down tables in the restaurant section, humming something completely out of tune and totally unrecognisable. More people came into the shop and Ed took their orders, all the while avoiding the questioning look Jo was giving him. She was dying to ask if the woman was his girlfriend – until she saw the diamond ring and the wedding band on the woman's left hand.

Jo felt as if she'd been slapped in the face with a wet fish, although she had no idea why. It didn't matter to her if Ed Fisher was a married man. They'd just shared a laugh, a bit of banter and a few bruises.

A couple of minutes later, Ed handed Jo a paper bag containing delicious smelling fish and chips wrapped in sheets of paper.

'That's on me,' he said.

Jo was about to offer to pay but for some reason she didn't. She gave him a quick smile, said thanks and marched away as quickly as she could.

Chapter Ten

Jo arrived at Wynter House shortly before lunch on Saturday. It still made her smile that everything ran to a timetable: breakfast between 8 and 9, lunch at 1, afternoon tea at 4 and drinks followed by dinner at 8 every day, even at weekends. She'd asked Rafe when she'd first arrived a few weeks ago whether this was because there were several guests staying from the village, but he'd given her a look as if he didn't understand her question.

'No. We always ate at these times, although we didn't generally have all our meals in the dining room, apart from dinner at the weekends when Adam would come home from London. Prior to us having guests, I'd often eat in the kitchen with Gavin and Archie during the week, or join Olivia in her rooms for supper. But that was when Penny and Taryn went to their respective homes in the evening. Now that we're all here, it makes sense to use the dining room.'

'So you still had afternoon tea at 4 every day, even when you didn't have guests?'

He'd furrowed his brows. 'Yes.'

'Do you ever have snacks? I mean, do you ever nip into the kitchen and make yourself a sandwich or something?'

'Penny makes such wonderful meals, there's really no need. But I suppose if I were particularly hungry, I might.'

'Do you know how to cook?'

He'd seemed surprised by that. 'Yes. Before Taryn joined us, I would often cook on Penny's day off. Although to be fair to Penny, she would usually leave something that Archie, Gavin or I could simply heat up. Why are you so interested in our eating habits?'

He had smiled, so he obviously wasn't irritated by her questions, but he'd missed the point. To him, the set timetable seemed perfectly normal. Jo wondered if he ever ordered pizza, or a takeaway. Even though he was dating Neva, he didn't seem much like an ordinary, everyday man. Certainly not the men Jo and Neva were used to dating. There was an air of formality about him and Jo wasn't sure if that was good or bad. If he and Neva married, Neva's life would become like his.

'Do you ever think about what it would be like to be Rafe's wife?' Jo asked Neva as they headed towards the dining room for lunch.

'Oh God yes. It would be wonderful. I know

we've only been dating since Christmas Eve, but I think about it all the time. I can't imagine my life without him now. It actually frightens me sometimes. Mainly on the few nights when I sleep at our flat. I wake up and panic about what I'll do if he stops loving me.'

'You've really got it bad, haven't you? But I don't think you need worry. He's clearly crazy about you. And didn't Adam tell you that, unlike himself, when Rafe falls for someone, you can pretty much guarantee he's in it for the long haul? Although from the way Adam looks at Hazel, I think he's more like Rafe than he wants to admit.'

'Yes. And I agree with you about Adam. But what if Rafe falls for someone else?'

Jo tutted. 'That's unlikely. Didn't both Rafe and Adam tell you that Rafe's only ever been in love with two women in his entire life? You, and his first wife, Pippa.'

Neva nodded and smiled. 'Yes. They both said that.'

'Well then. He's not the type of guy who falls in and out of love, is he? And as it took him most of his adult life to get over Pippa, he's not going to fall out of love with you in a hurry. The only thing you might have to worry about is if Pippa ever came back. And that's not going to happen, is it?'

'Oh my God! I hadn't even thought of that. What if she does?'

Jo wished she hadn't mentioned it.

'Oh come on, Neva. It was a joke. There's more chance of me marrying Gavin than there is of Rafe's first wife coming back. She had an affair and broke his heart. Then she left him. And didn't he say when you first met that he didn't hear a word from her for five years? You told me some people even believed he'd murdered her because she disappeared so suddenly. Then out of the blue, she sent him divorce papers. And now it's been another fourteen years. She's hardly likely to pull up on the drive one day and come for afternoon tea, is she? And even if she did – which she won't – but if she did, he's not going to welcome her with open arms. You don't do that to people who shatter your heart into tiny pieces.'

Neva smiled tentatively. 'No. You're right. I'm being silly. It's just that I love him so much, Jo. I really do.'

'I know. But as I said earlier, have you thought about what it'd be like to be his wife? And I don't mean all the lovely-dovey good bits and the great sex and the hearts and flowers stuff. I mean your day-to-day life. You'd be living in a house which is more like a museum. I'm not saying it's not a warm and welcoming place because it is. And it would be more so if you removed Olivia completely. But it's not exactly your normal family home, is it? We can walk around our flat naked if we want. You could never do that here. You'd never know when Carruthers, or Judith, or Penny, or Taryn, or Gavin might pop up. Although I wouldn't mind Gavin popping up if I were naked.'

Neva tutted and slapped her arm. 'Do you ever stop thinking about sex?'

'Never. I can't help myself. Although when I was staying here and George was teaching me about nature and stuff, I was thinking about it less. Perhaps I should spend more time with George. Anyway. Answer the question. Have you considered what your life would be like as Mrs Neva Wynter?'

'Yes. And I can see why you're asking that. The thought of having staff and running a big house like this had never occurred to me until I met Rafe. The odd thing is, although it's pretty daunting in so many ways, it's also rather exciting. And as weird as it sounds, it's not that much different from when I lived at home. Obviously, I didn't have staff, and our house in Surrey was about one hundredth of the size of this place. But I never ran around naked there either because Mum and Dad, or Rowan might have friends popping in and out, and when Rowan started dating Nigel, he was always coming and going at all times of the day and night. What I'm saying is, this house is no different to that, in a way. Just much, much bigger. And instead of Mum and Dad doing all the cooking, cleaning, repairs and gardening, people here are paid to do it. But they're more like family or really good friends than staff, especially since everyone's had to live here due to the village flooding.'

Jo thought about that for a second. 'That's true, I suppose. But if you married someone normal it'd only be you and him until you had kids. Here, you'll never, ever be alone. Doesn't that bother you?'

'Strangely enough, it doesn't. But are you saying Rafe's not normal?' Neva laughed.

As they walked into the dining room, Rafe, Gavin and Adam were each straining on long lengths of rope while Carruthers stood, somewhat precariously, Jo thought, atop a very tall step ladder, guiding one of the chandeliers into position.

'Oh hello,' Rafe said, beaming at Neva and Jo. 'Sorry about this. We'll only be a few more minutes. Polishing and rehanging the crystals took a little longer than expected.'

'I'm not saying anything of the sort,' Jo whispered, a hint of amusement in her voice. 'Because polishing and rehanging the crystals on a seven-foot long, ornate chandelier that takes four grown men to put it back in place, is a perfectly normal way to spend a Saturday morning.'

Chapter Eleven

'It's official,' Jo announced the following day. 'All men are bastards.'

Neva and Hazel were waiting at the door of Wynter House. The three of them were going for a Sunday afternoon stroll around the grounds. It was the sort of thing the girlfriends of the Wynter brothers should do, Neva had joked after Sunday lunch, when Rafe and Adam, together with Sean, said they were going to do a couple of things in the distillery. Neva and Hazel, along with Jo, had offered to help but Rafe had tactfully told them that it would take longer to explain what to do, than it would for the three men to just get on and do it. Although he'd had the sense to add that they'd welcome help another time.

'Apart from Rafe,' Neva said. 'Oh, and Adam, of course.'

Hazel grinned. 'I'm not sure about Adam. I think he could still be bit of a bastard, given the right circumstances.'

'Really?' Neva was surprised by that, but Hazel simply nodded.

'All the men I fall for are,' Jo said, as they walked away from the house. 'Listen to this.' She held up her phone and read from the screen. "I sent it to you by mistake. It was meant for someone else. All sorted now. Unlikely to ever be down your way but I'll give you a bell if I am. Rob." That's it. No apology. No, "But I do miss you." No kisses. Nothing.'

'I thought Rob was your ex-fiancé,' Hazel said.

'He is. But I got a sexy-sounding text on Monday and I thought he wanted me back. Not that I want him back. Except to have sex. I miss having sex. Anyway, Neva and I discussed it and then I thought about it and I texted him on Thursday saying I was surprised to get his text. That I'm loving life here. That I hoped he was happy and that if he was down this way at any time in the near future, he could give me a call. The bastard has only just replied and he's basically telling me that, not only is he already having sex with someone else – and not just sex but great sex – but that he doesn't care if he never sees me again.'

Neva linked her arm through Jo's. 'I'm so sorry, Jo. But at least now you know.'

'But he waited three days to reply,' Hazel said. 'I know it took you three days to get back to him but that's not the point.'

'I know, right? What a git.' Jo tutted loudly.

Hazel stopped in her tracks and Neva and Jo did likewise.

'You should text him back right now,' Hazel said. 'Say something like, 'Phew. I was worried you wanted me back and I didn't want to hurt your feelings. Glad you're seeing someone. Hope she's as fantastic as the sexy, rich hunk I'm dating. Sending this from his front garden. Everything about this man is huge!' Put 'huge' in capitals then take a photo of these grounds, with the house in the background and send it to him with some appropriate emojis. A thumbs up, bulging eyes, a couple of ones with a tongue hanging out, oh, and a pot of gold. And maybe a couple of those mouths with red lipstick ones. That should knock every aspect of his self-esteem. Men hate to think you're dating someone better looking, better endowed, better in bed, wealthier, and more successful than them.'

Neva and Jo looked at one another in astonishment.

'Wow!' Jo said, her fingers hovering over her phone. 'Can you repeat that word for word?'

Hazel did. And Jo sent it along with a photo of the house.

'Why do I get the impression you've done this before?' Neva asked.

Hazel grinned and shrugged before

becoming serious.

'About a year before I came here, I broke up with my long-term boyfriend. We'd been dating for several years and although he said he loved me, he would never take things to the next level. We lived in separate houses, but we spent most of our time together, when he wasn't out and about with all his mates. He's a policeman and very sporty. He's also into motorbikes and loves taking them apart and doing them up. Anyway, eventually I gave him an ultimatum. I told him that unless he would commit to us moving in together I felt we should end our relationship. I know that probably wasn't a sensible thing to do, but a girl can only wait so long. I want to have children before I'm forty and if that wasn't going to be with him, I needed time to meet someone else, build a good and solid relationship and give myself time to become a mum.'

'And he said no, I take it,' Jo said. 'Bloody men.'

Hazel nodded. 'But not right away. He said he needed time to think. Although what was there to think about? We'd been together for eight years and we'd known each other for several years before that. I gave him more time and we did go and view a couple of houses. But he was always saying they weren't quite right. I finally realised it was never going to happen. We had a blazing row and I stormed out of the restaurant he'd taken me to for my birthday. I thought he'd call but he didn't. A couple of months later, I heard he'd started seeing someone and I knew I had to get over him. Which I have. But he sent me a text the day before I came here to wish me a happy birthday. Just that. Nothing else. It just said, "Happy Birthday, Hazel. Jason." As ridiculous as I thought it was at the time, the first evening I was here, I typed a text back, thanking him and saying I hadn't replied right away because I'd been with my new boyfriend, staying at his ancestral home. I added that he'd done me a favour by not wanting to commit because I was now with a gorgeous man who did. And I hate to admit this, but I sent it.'

'Good for you,' Jo said.

'But the thing is, I don't like lying. Honesty is something I feel very strongly about. And yet when it comes to ex-boyfriends, it seems I have no morals and no scruples. Honesty may be very important, but sadly to me, revenge is more so.'

'As it turned out,' Neva said, 'you weren't lying about Adam. It was more of a premonition, in fact. Because you are staying at the ancestral home of your new boyfriend. But I didn't know it was your birthday the day before you arrived. We would've baked you a belated birthday cake or something to make you feel more welcome.'

'Birthdays aren't important to me. The older I get the more I'd like to forget them. And as for making me feel welcome, I've never felt more welcome anywhere than you all made me feel the first day I was here.'

'Even Olivia?' Neva grinned at her.

'Well, maybe not Olivia. But definitely everyone else.'

'That's the thing about this place,' Neva said. 'You feel at home the minute you walk through the door. You feel as if you belong here. Even Olivia can't dampen the welcome, as hard as she may try.'

'I feel as if I belong here with Gavin,' Jo said. 'If only Gavin felt the same.'

Chapter Twelve

Neva couldn't believe her eyes when Cat and Kyra finally lay down their brushes after almost a week of working on the trompe l'oeil in the salon. She and Jo had seen the painting develop a little more each day, and had marvelled at Cat and Kyra's talent, but to see the artwork completed was still a wonderful surprise. It was even better than Neva had imagined. And she had imagined something very special indeed.

This exceeded all her expectations and it was clear Jo felt the same. Especially when Cat and Kyra flatly refused to take any money for their work, saying it had been such a pleasure for them and that they were giving it to Neva and Jo as a moving in cum opening gift. Neva had already offered to give Cat and Kyra some complimentary haircuts and beauty treatments, and at least they did agree to accept those.

Neva and Jo were more than a little

emotional as they hugged and kissed Cat and Kyra; before long, they were all weeping tears of joy. Jo suggested champagne, and dashed to The Merry Shopper supermarket, returning fifteen minutes or so later with three bottles of bubbly and some cakes.

They raised several glasses to the trompe l'oeil and then to other things, like life and love and family. They also toasted their new-found friendship.

'It's the Merriment Bay Moonlight Valentine's Dance on Friday,' Neva said as the four of them sat on the large, multi-coloured sofa in the salon. 'I can't do anything on the actual day, 'cos Rafe and I are doing something special. No idea what, 'cos he hasn't told me. He wants it to be a surprise.' She gave a little hiccough. She had drunk more than she had intended. 'But I can do something on Thursday. That's the day before. Tomorrow, in fact. For you and for Kyra and also for your mum, if you like. It'll be a dry run for us to see whether everything in the salon works as it should before we open for business. I want everything to be perfect.'

Jo made a joke about her glass being dry and held it upside down to prove the point, but she also agreed about the dry run, which Cat and Kyra drunkenly and gratefully accepted.

Neva couldn't really recall much of what they talked about after that.

Jo had mentioned lusting after Gavin, but had said he wasn't interested. She hadn't mentioned Rob, other than to say something along the lines of getting engaged and moving in together was a mistake. And Cat had told them it had taken Amias more than eighteen years to tell her he'd loved her all his life.

'I don't want to wait eighteen years,' Jo had said. 'I haven't had sex since before Christmas.'

'You could ask him out,' Kyra said.

'You could ask him to marry you,' Neva said, although she had no idea why. 'It's a leap year. Women can propose to men on leap years.'

Kyra tutted. 'Women can propose to men on any day of any year. But not many do. So much for equality. Why is that? Why do most women wait to be asked?'

'Because it's romantic,' Neva said. 'I'd rather be asked than ask. But Kyra's right, Jo. You could ask Gavin out.'

'I asked Amias,' Cat said, trying to sit upright but failing. 'I asked him how he felt about me. It was on New Year's Eve and we've been together ever since. He took me home to his beautiful house and we made wonderful love all night and again in the morning and every day afterwards.'

Kyra told Cat that was too much information.

Neva told them how much she loved Rafe,

87

and the others all repeated who they loved. Even Kyra thought she might have fallen for someone but she wasn't completely sure.

And then Cat had surprised them all, including herself by the look on her face, by announcing she was going to propose to Amias at the Merriment Bay Moonlight Valentine's Dance.

'Are you sure, Mum?' Kyra queried. 'I mean, I think you proposing is a fantastic idea, but at the dance? Wouldn't you rather do it somewhere more romantic?'

'A dance is romantic,' Jo said. 'At least if it's done right it is. I think it'll be brilliant.'

'Me too,' said Neva. 'I wish I'd thought of that. I think I'd quite like to ask Rafe to marry me. We haven't known each other very long but time doesn't matter, does it? It's how we feel that's important.'

Jo nodded. 'That's what we've been saying all night, isn't it?'

'Have we?' Neva couldn't really remember. 'Well, that's good, because it's true. So how are you going to do it, Cat? Will you get down on one knee?'

Kyra tutted. 'Please don't do that, Mum. I'm begging you. If you're serious about this, please find another way to ask. I don't think a woman should effectively beg a man to marry her.'

'Men get down on one knee,' Jo said.

'I know. But that's different. That's a sign of respect. That's a man saying he's forgetting all about his ego and showing the world how much he wants the woman to be his wife. A man doing that is seen as a sign of true love. A woman doing that is seen as desperation. Sorry, but it is.'

Jo nodded. 'I see your point. It shouldn't be different, but it is. So how should your mum do it then? If she can't go down on one knee.'

'I could ask Natalia?' Cat said.

Jo grinned. 'I think she's already married. And I thought you were proposing to Amias?'

'Don't be an idiot.' Neva nudged Jo's arm. 'Cat wasn't saying she was going to propose to Natalia. Were you?'

'Of course not,' Cat said. 'But she knows her brother better than anyone so she'll have some advice about how I should go about it. I'm going to call her right now and ask her.'

'It's late, Mum,' Kyra said, pointing at the clock on the wall as if she couldn't quite decipher the time.

'Then I'll call her and ask her to come round tomorrow to discuss it.'

'Why don't you ask her to come here?' Neva said. 'That way we can all get involved. And tell her we'll do her hair for her too.'

'Are you sure?' Cat asked, holding the phone to her ear.

'Absolutely. We'd be delighted. And that

way Jo and I will get to hear about your plans for your proposal.'

'That sounds perfect,' Cat said. 'Natalia! It's Cat. I need your advice.'

'And I need a drink,' Jo said, as Cat told Natalia of her plan.

Chapter Thirteen

Neva spent most of Thursday drinking black coffee and nursing a hangover whilst cutting and styling the hair of all the women staying at Wynter House, with the exception of Olivia. So by the time she got back to the salon, Cat, Kyra, Mary and Natalia were already there, drinking coffee with Jo.

Neva and Jo had intended to make a little party of it, but everyone except Mary and Natalia were also nursing hangovers from the previous day, so a party was the last thing any of them felt like having. Neva had told Hazel that she could join them, but Hazel had already made plans with Adam and was reluctant to cancel, so Neva had cut and styled Hazel's hair before leaving Wynter House.

'Aren't you worn out?' Cat asked. 'I'm exhausted and I've done nothing very much all day.'

'I am a bit tired. But I love my job,' Neva said. 'And I love bringing out the best in people's looks. A good haircut can do wonders sometimes. You should see what I've done with Judith. She's Rafe and Olivia's P.A., Natalia. I don't know if you know her but anyway. Half the people at Wynter House didn't recognise her when I'd finished. I did her hair at Christmas but this time she let me colour it. And it's made a huge difference.'

Jo poured her a glass of champagne. 'Hair of the dog. And besides, we're sort of celebrating the fact that Cat is going to propose to Amias. That calls for champagne.'

Neva pulled a face. 'It does, I agree. But I'm only having one glass. It's Valentine's Day tomorrow and I want to be bright-eyed and bushy tailed for my romantic day out with Rafe.'

'Has he told you what he's got planned?' Cat asked.

'No. It's still a secret. I did wonder if he doesn't have anything planned and is delaying in the hope he'll think of something before tomorrow, but that's probably just me. If I had something planned, I don't think I could keep it a secret. But whatever it is, I don't mind. I'll just be blissfully happy to spend an entire day with the man I adore.'

'Dear God,' said Jo. 'I really need a drink.'

'So what's the plan for the proposal then?' Neva said, sipping her champagne, after slapping Jo on the arm.

'OK', said Cat. 'What we've come up with so far is that Taryn Small will sing. I mean she's singing at the dance anyway, but we need to ask her to sing a couple of special songs for this to work. Jo said you would ask her, Neva, because you know her better than anyone else does.'

'I'll be happy to ask her. And she's lovely so I know she'll say yes. But if they're songs she doesn't know, you may need to give her a bit of time to rehearse them. I'll call her in a moment and we can see what she says. But let's assume it's all OK and she knows the songs. What's next?'

'She'll sing, 'Be My Lucky Valentine', to give me time to prepare and then she'll ask everyone to clear the floor but I'll pretend my heel is caught and I'll hold on to Amias until it's just him and me left standing there. Then I'll do a little speech. Which I'll need to write tomorrow. And, if he says yes. Oh God he must say yes. He will. I'm sure he will. So he'll say yes and then heart-shaped, red balloons will drop from the sky. Well, not from the sky. From netting hanging from the ceiling. Natalia says she can organise that. And Taryn will sing our favourite song, 'Maybe This Time' by Michael Murphy. The words are so apt. And we'll dance and then everyone will join us and ... that's it. That's all we've got for now.'

Neva and Jo both sighed.

'That is so romantic,' Neva said.

'It's also a bit terrifying,' Cat added. 'I hope I don't get nervous and make a complete and total mess of it.'

'How can you make a mess of asking the man you love to marry you?' Natalia said. 'Now if it was my darling brother doing the proposing and planning this, I'd be worried. He probably would make a complete pig's ear of the thing. But it's not him, it's you. And you'll do it perfectly. Just like you did on New Year's Eve. Look how well that turned out. You've been together ever since.'

'You're right, Natalia.' Cat sat upright. 'I can do this.'

Jo emptied the contents of her glass in one long gulp.

'Then Neva and I just need to make sure you look even more beautiful than you do already. So let's get started, shall we?'

Chapter Fourteen

Rain was forecast for Valentine's Day but thankfully not until the evening. Rain might not have put a damper on whatever Rafe had planned but Neva was glad that the sun was shining and the sky was clear when Rafe brought her breakfast in bed.

He'd put a single red rose in what she recognised as a Lalique crystal vase. She had come to learn quite a lot about antiques and expensive, sometimes priceless items since coming to Wynter House, but her meagre knowledge of Lalique was due to the fact it was her mum's favourite. She knew it varied in price from a few hundred pounds to the thousands and while she wasn't sure where this vase was on that scale, she was very glad that Rafe removed it from the breakfast tray and put it on the bedside table.

There was orange juice, champagne, English muffins cut into heart shapes topped with smoked salmon and poached eggs covered in Hollandaise sauce – a variation of Eggs Benedict – together with a Valentine card. Neva reached over and pulled a card for Rafe from her handbag which she'd left beside the bed, and when they opened them together, they laughed.

'Happy Valentine's Day!' Rafe said. 'I can't believe we got one another exactly the same card.'

When Neva told Jo about that later, she said that proved they were meant to be together, but Jo somewhat unromantically pointed out that what it really proved was that The Merry Shopper in Merriment Bay needed to increase their selection of Valentine's Day cards.

After breakfast, and rather a long time spent in the shower due to Rafe suggesting they shower together, they headed downstairs, hand in hand. Gavin appeared in the hall, looking somewhat flustered but before he could say a word, Rafe said that unless someone was dying – or even if they were – he trusted Gavin or Archie to deal with whatever disaster had occurred. Although he did wait until Gavin had confirmed that he could handle it. When Neva asked Rafe, much later, what it was, he grinned and said it was nothing to worry about. Merely another tree that had fallen down on the estate. This one, unlike the one just before Christmas, had only taken down a greenhouse, not the electricity supply.

Rafe didn't tell Neva until the very last minute what the surprise was he had planned. In fact, he never got to tell her. She saw it for herself as they drove towards the field that led to Wyntersleap Falls.

Her eyes opened wide and she shrieked with delight.

'Oh Rafe! Is that a hot air balloon? Are we going up in that?'

'Yes to both questions.'

'But balloon flights aren't cheap. This is too much, Rafe.' She tried to keep the excitement from her voice but she failed.

'It didn't cost me anything. The pilot's a good friend of mine. We do one another favours from time to time.'

'Oh wow! That makes it even better.'

He parked in the field just a few feet from where a team of people were busy preparing the balloon, and a very handsome man around Rafe's age, wearing a flying jacket, stepped forward to greet them.

'Hi,' he said with an easy smile. 'I'm Rory. You must be Neva. It's lovely to meet you. You're even prettier than Rafe said.' He winked at Rafe and slapped him on the shoulder. 'Great to see you again, mate. Thanks for the gin, by the way. You're onto a winner there.'

'It's good to see you too. I'm pleased to hear the gin went down well. Let me know when you want more.' He smiled at Rory and wrapped his arm around Neva. 'Rory and I went to uni together, but he's also a friend of Amias'. He lives a few miles away in Eastbourne and runs a company providing balloon flights, amongst other adventure experiences.'

'Wow. It's lovely to meet you,' Neva said. If Rafe had told her about this, and how gorgeous Rory was, she would've asked if Jo could come along and watch.

'I think we're going to be lucky with the weather,' Rory said. 'And the prevailing winds are perfect. We should be able to fly over Wyntersleap Falls, down to Little Wynter Falls and Wyntersleap reservoir and on to Merriment Bay. From there we'll be able to hug the coast without drifting out to sea, I hope.' He winked again at Neva. 'We may have to make a rapid descent if we veer off course. It's no fun landing in the sea at the best of times, especially not in February.'

Neva glanced nervously from Rory to Rafe but neither men looked concerned.

'We've made a start,' Rory said, 'but if you'd like to give us a hand that would be great.'

'Tell us where you want us,' Rafe said.

'OK. As you can see, the envelope – that's the big balloon-shaped bit, is attached to the basket, or gondola, as we like to call it. It's on its side and attached to one of our Land Rovers.

We don't want it taking off without us. Two of my ground crew are standing either side of the mouth of the balloon and we're using high-powered fans to fill the envelope with cold air. The others are spreading it out, while another stands at the other end and holds the crown line. That keeps the top of the balloon down near the ground while it's being inflated. Why don't you go and hold the crown line, Rafe, and Neva, you take Sharon's place at the mouth. That way you'll be closer to me if anything happens.'

'Is anything likely to happen?' Neva was nervous again.

Rory grinned. 'No. I'd just prefer to look at your face rather than Rafe's. I'll get one of my crew to take plenty of photos for you. It may get a bit noisy as I prepare the burners. But it won't take long for them to heat the air and that'll create the lift while I do some final safety and weather checks. When the balloon starts to rise, it's really important you hold that crown line firm, Rafe. But I'll get Paul to step in and take over so that you and Neva can get in once the balloon is upright. I'll ask you to take your landing positions in the gondola. That means sitting on the bench seat and holding the leather-covered rope handles. Don't grab any of the other ropes while getting in or out, and when we land, I'll need you both to keep your arms and legs inside, so we'll do a quick practice of that. Then I'll use the burners to increase the temperature of the air in the envelope and when I'm happy with that, I'll pull the quick release and detach us from the Land Rover. If I forget to do that, please remind me. We don't want to be dragging that across the fields and over the Falls instead of drifting serenely up into this beautiful clear blue sky.'

'Don't worry, Neva,' Rafe said. 'He's joking.'

Rory grinned. 'I need to give you both a quick safety briefing. I'm the pilot. Obey me at all times. Don't grab anything other than the rigid leather-covered uprights, and the leather-covered handles inside. You can grab me, Neva, if you're scared. Rafe, you're on your own. Stay away from those inflator fans. When we take off, don't lean over the side and definitely don't fall out. It'll hurt. It's my job to spot any obstacles or potential hazards, but if you see we're heading towards power lines, phone masts or anything else during take-off and landing, casually mention them to me, just in case I haven't spotted them. OK. That's it. Let's get this baby flying.'

Rafe ran to the crown line and took hold of it and Neva took Sharon's place at the mouth. But it wasn't long before Rory was calling them to get into the gondola and within a matter of minutes, Neva's tummy did a little flip as the balloon lifted off the grass and gently floated into the air.

Rafe wrapped his arm around her and they marvelled at the view as they soared over Wyntersleap Falls, still majestic but not quite as terrifying as they'd been the first time she'd seen them. They coasted towards Little Wynter Falls and then flew over the reservoir.

'Is that Amias on the reservoir with a pupil?' Rafe said. 'I'm sure he told us he had a paddle boarding lesson booked today.'

They yelled and waved and the people below them looked up and waved back, but it didn't look like Amias.

Approaching Merriment Bay was magical, with the sun still hung low over the horizon and not a cloud in the sky. Rory turned off one of the burners and used what he told them was the 'whisper burner', which let out the propane more slowly, making it quieter.

It was chilly up there, far above the fields and the houses, but the heat from the burners kept Neva's head and shoulders warm and toasty and the coat Rafe had insisted she wear, kept the rest of her at a comfortable temperature. Plus she was wrapped in Rafe's arms for much of the time, apart from when they were taking photos, so that helped.

Rory hardly said a word, unless she or Rafe asked him a question. He was fun and flirty on the ground, but once they were on their flight it was as if he wanted them to feel they were alone, just the two of them and the elements, drifting across the sky, although he took a fantastic photo of them with the sun behind them, like a giant halo.

He'd told them that an average balloon flight would cover between five and ten miles, depending on the wind. Merriment Bay was exactly five miles from Wyntersleap village, and about six from the field where they'd taken off. Rory began to give them landing instructions about a mile along the coast past Merriment Bay. Neva couldn't believe they'd been in the air for an hour, but they had, and Rory brought the balloon down safely and smoothly in a field.

Neva was surprised to see the chase crew were ready and waiting but they only got out of their Land Rovers when the balloon was a few feet from the ground.

'That was sensational,' Neva said, hugging and kissing Rafe. 'I've never experienced anything like it. Thank you from the bottom of my heart.' She was so emotional she had to fight back tears of joy.

Rafe looked ecstatic. 'I'm so pleased you enjoyed it. I know I did.' He kissed her as if he'd forgotten they were in company and everyone clapped and cheered.

'Thank you, Rory.' He smiled at his friend. 'You're the best. I owe you big time.'

'It was my pleasure, Rafe. After everything

you've done for me, I still owe you.'

The crew swung into action and as Rory poured champagne and took some more photos of Neva and Rafe, the balloon was being deflated. It took less than thirty minutes and a little while after that, the balloon and the basket, or gondola, were neatly packed away.

'This is probably a silly idea, Rafe,' Neva said, watching the final strap being fixed in place, 'but what do you think about having this hot air balloon in the grounds of Wynter House for the official launch of Wyntersleap Gin? Perhaps, if it's tethered to the ground, the press and buyers could go up a few feet in it and then come back down. They would be able to see all the way to Merriment Bay and they could see Wyntersleap Falls, which is where you say on the bottle you get your water from. Or you could ask Kyra to pose in the basket with a glass of gin for the brochure. She's stunning and her long ginger hair would look sensational in the right breeze. You could say, 'Wyntersleap Gin is the perfect refreshment for high flyers,' or something along those lines.'

Rafe and Rory stared at her.

'Sorry,' she added. 'I said it was a silly idea.'

'It's a brilliant idea,' Rafe said, putting down his glass and lifting her into the air in his arms.

'I agree,' Rory said, beaming. 'It is.'

Rafe set Neva down and kissed her before

glancing at Rory and smiling.

'But this time you'll be paid. Don't argue. Wyntersleap Gin is a business and this is a business transaction. Let's sort out some suitable dates and I'll run it past Sean and Adam. They'll agree, I'm sure. None of us has come up with anything as good as Neva's idea. I'm not sure if Kyra will agree but there's no harm in asking.'

'Let's drink to that,' Rory said, refilling Neva and Rafe's glasses. 'But we'll talk about payment at a later date because, if the press is there, I'll get lots of free publicity. Who knows, I might even get some bookings.'

'I'll drink to that,' Rafe said.

'I'll drink to you both.' Neva raised her glass in the air. 'And to Love. It *is* Valentine's Day, after all.'

'To Love,' Rafe and Rory said in unison.

'And to you, my darling Neva.'

Rafe raised his glass and blew her a kiss and the look in his eyes sent her heart soaring.

Chapter Fifteen

The Merriment Bay Moonlight Valentine's Dance was held in the main assembly hall of St Mary's School, which was in the centre of Merriment Bay, opposite the church of St Mary-in-the-Fields. The church was built in 1069 in the middle of open fields, and the village had sprung up around it. Constance Raine, the vicar's wife, along with other members of the Merriment Bay W.I. had organised the dance for more than twenty years, but this year Cat, Kyra and Mary Devon had been brought on board to help.

The hall was festooned with heart-shaped bunting and during the dance, heart-shaped, red balloons dropped from the sky. Only not to Cat and Amias' favourite song as originally planned.

Cat had chickened out.

Neva received a frantic call from Cat as she and Rafe were getting ready.

'I can't do it, Neva. I've been thinking

about it for the entire day. Amias had lessons booked for most of the day. He'd tried to cancel them but he hadn't been able to contact some of the pupils. I don't know why I'm telling you that except to say that he came home feeling very tired. I'm not sure he's in the right frame of mind for a marriage proposal. But more importantly, I'm definitely not in the right frame of mind to make it. Can you speak to Taryn, please and cancel everything? Oh, and can she sing something other than our favourite song when the balloons fall? Amias might think there's something strange going on if he hears our song when that happens.'

'Oh! Er. Yes of course. I'll have a word with Taryn right now. I'm sure she'll think of another song. Don't worry about a thing. Leave it with me. But are you absolutely sure you don't want to do it? I think it is so romantic.'

'Yes. I'm sure. I've spoken to Natalia and she agrees it's for the best if my nerves are getting to me. She says it might not come out right and then we'd both be disappointed. Oh. But how was your day? What was Rafe's surprise?'

'Oh, Cat. It was wonderful. We went up in a hot air balloon. It was magical. The best Valentine's Day I've ever had. And I do mean ever. But I'd better go and get ready. I'll see you at the dance. And don't worry. I'll handle everything with Taryn.'

'What are you handling with Taryn?' Rafe asked, returning after a summons from Olivia.

'Nothing. I mean, nothing much. Cat was going to ask her to sing a special song, but now she thinks Amias might feel funny about it so she's asked me to ask Taryn not to sing it. Which I'm going to do right now. What did Olivia want?'

Rafe grinned. 'She saw the hot air balloon and she wanted to know why it seemed to be flying over our land and whether I'd given permission for it to be inflated in one of our fields.'

Neva grinned. 'I bet she wasn't pleased when you told her.'

'Let's just say she had a few choice words to say about people doing the silliest things in the so-called name of Love, but she was a little less irritated when I told her it hadn't cost me a penny.'

Neva had spoken to Taryn and Taryn hadn't been at all concerned. When the balloons came down, she sang 'Ninety-nine Red Balloons', instead.

Food and drink were plentiful with all the sale proceeds going to local charities. Neva and Rafe danced together for most of the night but Rafe also danced with Jo a few times, as did Adam and Amias. Neva knew the person Jo really wanted to dance with; the problem was, it seemed he didn't want to dance with her. Jo kept making a beeline for Gavin and he kept hurrying away. He did dance with her once or twice but he mainly danced with Judith. They'd worked together at Wynter House for years and had been friends from the beginning, so Rafe told Neva, so the poor man obviously felt safe with Judith. Gavin didn't appear to be a man who liked to be chased.

The dance ended in the early hours, and everyone made their way home in the pouring rain. But it had been forecast, so no one could say they were surprised by the weather, especially as it was February.

'This has been the perfect day,' Neva said, trying not to slur her words. She had drunk rather a lot more at the dance than she'd intended and what with the champagne for breakfast and the champagne after the balloon flight, she was definitely a little plastered.

'It's not over yet,' Adam said.

He and Hazel, Judith and Gavin were all in the taxi together with Neva and Rafe. They'd booked one of those large people carriers that could seat eight. Neva had expected Jo to return with them to Wynter House but she asked to be dropped at the flat in Merriment Bay instead. She'd said she would walk as it was only a few minutes from the hall, but Rafe wouldn't hear of that. Neva had tried to convince her to go with them, but Jo was adamant. She wanted to stay at the flat. Neva offered to stay there too, so that Jo wouldn't be alone but Jo got cross and told her not to be so silly.

'Go with Rafe and enjoy a night of mad, passionate sex. I'm going home to bed. Call me in the morning. But not too early. Not before ten at least.'

Rafe got out and opened the door to the flat; he waited until Jo was safely inside before the rest of them continued to Wynter House.

'I wish Jo could find a man to love her as much as you love me,' Neva said, leaning against Rafe.

'She will. She's fun. She's pretty. She's a lovely person. She just needs to wait until the right man comes along.'

'Don't you like her, Gavin?' Neva asked.

Gavin shot a look at Judith. 'Yes. As a friend. But not in a romantic way.'

'Have you ever been in love?' Neva persisted.

Rafe tutted good-naturedly. 'Leave the man alone, Neva.'

'I'm only asking. Everyone should be in love. Being in love is wonderful. Why aren't you in love, Gavin?'

'I am.'

Even Rafe looked surprised by that, as did Adam. But not as surprised as Gavin. He clearly hadn't meant to say that.

Neva sat upright. 'You are? Who with?'

Rafe's tone was a little more serious. 'Neva, it's really none of our business.'

'I had no idea,' Adam said.

'Is it someone we know?' Neva couldn't stop now. 'Judith? Do you know who the lucky lady is?'

Oddly, Judith seemed upset and hastily looked away. 'Gavin hasn't told me.'

Neva looked from one to the other and then she looked at Hazel.

'Do you know who it is, Hazel? Because from the way Gavin's looking at Judith, I'm getting the feeling that it might be her. And from the expression on her face, I believe she feels the same about him. What do you think?'

Judith gasped. Gavin swore. Rafe tutted loudly. Adam also swore and then laughed. Hazel nodded in agreement.

'I think you're right.'

Then everyone fell silent and stared at Judith and Gavin.

'Well, this is rather embarrassing,' Gavin said, after a moment or two.

'See.' Neva pointed at him. 'He's not denying it. He loves you, Judith!'

Judith turned the colour of blood and she seemed to be shaking.

'You can't. You don't. We've worked together for years and you've never said a word. Tonight, when you kept asking me to dance, I thought there might be some hope that you really liked me, but love? It's not true, is it? If you loved me you would've told me.'

Her statements were more like questions and as they looked at one another it was as if they forgot everyone else was there.

'I know you don't feel the same, so I've kept it to myself.'

'You mean it's true?' Her voice was a high-pitched squeal.

'Of course it's true!'

Neva screamed in delight. 'It's the hair! I knew that colour made you more beautiful. And it made Gavin realise you were beautiful too and he suddenly fell in love with you.'

'Neva.' Rafe pulled her to him and grinned. 'Keep out of this, please.'

Gavin gave a slow smile and shook his head.

'It's not your hair. Although it does suit you. I suppose I may as well say it now. I've loved you for years. I'm not sure when it started but one day I looked at you and I realised I didn't just like you. I loved you. But I thought you were in love with someone else, so I kept quiet and then I'd kept it to myself for so long that it didn't seem as if I'd ever be able to say it. I'm only saying it now because I've had too much to drink and part of me is hoping none of us will remember this tomorrow.'

Judith reached out and took his hand in hers.

'I'll remember it tomorrow, Gavin. It's a dream come true. I can't say it's been years for me, but it's definitely been a while. And if you forget what you said tonight, I'll remind you over breakfast.'

They gazed into each other's eyes and everyone stared at them and at one another.

'May I say something now?' Neva asked. 'I think you should kiss Judith, Gavin. We'll all look away if you want some privacy.'

He may or may not have heard her, but he kissed Judith anyway. And everyone did look away, except for Neva, until Rafe took her face in his hands, turned her around and kissed her.

Chapter Sixteen

Neva woke up with a thumping headache and as she turned over in bed, she realised Rafe wasn't there. Perhaps he'd gone to make coffee. She really needed some. She also needed some headache tablets.

Those she had, and she reached down beside the bed for her handbag. She managed to push herself upright, or at least almost, and poured herself some water from the glass carafe on the bedside table.

And that's when she saw it.

She was wearing Rafe's signet ring.

On the third finger of her left hand.

It was a perfect fit. But that wasn't what mattered.

What mattered was why exactly was she wearing it?

He had told her once when she'd asked that he'd been given it for his eighteenth birthday by Olivia and he had never taken it off. Adam had one too. And he'd laughed and also smiled with pride when he told her what the inscription on the inside said. "Wynters leap, where others fear to tread". It was a play on words and a nod not only to the Wynter family and their supposed courage, but also to their ancestors who leapt from Wyntersleap Falls, and to the village of Wyntersleap itself. It meant a great deal to him.

So why had he taken it off last night?

And why had he put it on her finger?

Her wedding finger.

Had Rafe proposed?

And if so, where was he right now?

What had happened last night?

She remembered the dance. She remembered the journey home.

Gavin had told Judith he loved her.

They'd all celebrated when they got back to Wynter House.

For several hours. And they all had much too much to drink.

Then Gavin had asked Judith on a date and Neva had overheard him and had said something like, 'Why waste time dating? You know each other better than most couples already. Why not just move in together?' But really as a joke.

Rafe had told her not to interfere but Judith had said it wasn't a bad idea and Gavin had said it was a very good idea. But that he had an even better one. He'd got down on one knee and asked her to marry him. And Judith had said yes.

Which had resulted in more celebrations.

Rafe suggested they could marry in the chapel at Wynter House if that appealed to them. Apparently, it did.

Then Neva had started thinking about how wonderful it would have been if Cat and Amias had also got engaged last night. If Cat hadn't lost her nerve. Perhaps Cat and Amias could have married in the chapel at Wynter House too. Neva imagined how romantic it would have been. From there she had gone on to picture what it would be like to have a wedding at Wynter House.

And then she remembered.

Gavin wasn't the only one who had proposed last night.

She stared at Rafe's signet ring and didn't know what to do.

Because now she remembered everything.

After she and Rafe had come upstairs and Rafe was getting undressed, she had knelt on the bed watching him ... and then she had proposed to him.

Except it hadn't actually been a proposal.

Yes, she had said, 'Will you marry me, Rafe?' But what she had meant to say was, 'Will you want to marry me one day? Is that where this relationship is definitely heading?' Not, 'Will you marry me?' as in, 'Will you be my husband and can we get engaged right now?'

But had he thought it was a drunken joke? Or had he taken it seriously?

She could vividly remember the two of them laughing and kissing. And she could remember him saying he didn't have a ring because this was a bit of a surprise. But then he'd said he did have a ring. The Wynter ring. And he had taken it off, with a bit of a struggle, and slipped it on her finger. And he had accepted her proposal.

Oh God. So he must've taken it seriously.

But if he had, where was he right now? Had he gone downstairs to make her another romantic breakfast?

Or had he had second thoughts now that he was sober? Was he avoiding her? Was he taking time to think and find a way to backtrack?

Had he gone out to buy her a ring?

He wouldn't have gone to Merriment Bay and left her in bed. That was silly.

She glanced at her watch. It was 10 a.m. She stared at it. 10 a.m! She never stayed in bed until 10, at least not on her own.

What should she do?

If he thought they were engaged, he'd say something, wouldn't he?

She leapt out of bed, ignoring her still pounding head, grabbed her dressing gown and ran to the bedroom door, yanking it open

... and careering into Rafe.

The tray fell out of his hands, spilling coffee, orange juice and champagne, along with a couple of Penny's delicious chocolate croissants, onto the ancient oak floor of the hall.

'What the ...? Where were you off to in such an almighty rush?'

Rafe looked both surprised and a little disappointed as he bent down to pick up the broken glass and crockery.

'I was coming to look for you.' Neva bent down to help him.

Carruthers appeared a second later.

'That was quick, Archie. You must have super powers. I always suspected as much.'

The butler's brows danced up and down and he seemed unusually flustered. He was definitely out of breath and he took a deep intake of air before he spoke.

'I wish I had, Rafe. But I never saw this one coming.'

Neva had never heard him speak in such a casual and pally manner, but she knew they probably did so out of earshot of everyone else.

Rafe stopped what he was doing and shot upright.

'What is it, Archie? What the hell has happened?'

Chapter Seventeen

'You have got to be kidding me.' Jo couldn't believe it. Her head was thumping and her mouth felt as if she'd eaten a badger, or possibly a skunk, but that was nothing compared to this.

'Believe me, Jo, I'm not. I wish to God I were.' Neva sounded miserable and maybe even furious.

'You're honestly telling me that the very thing we talked about, laughed about, and none of us ever thought could possibly happen, has happened. Rafe's first wife has turned up. Completely out of the blue.'

'Yep. And the timing couldn't have been better. I proposed to him last night. Although I hadn't meant it as a proposal but he might have taken it seriously. At least I think he did because I woke up wearing his signet ring and he was bringing me breakfast in bed and we were picking up the pieces when Carruthers came and told us Phyllida was in the hall.

That's her real name. Pippa's. And–'

'Whoa! Slow down, Neva. What was that bit about you proposing to Rafe?'

Neva tutted. 'I told you. I proposed to him last night but I hadn't meant it as a proposal, just a theoretical question. You know, like as in, 'Will you marry me … one day in the future?'

'No. Sorry. You're not my type. But thanks for asking.'

'What? This isn't bloody funny, Jo. This is a mess. And the worst part is, the woman is drop dead gorgeous.'

'So? You said that about Amelia Goodbody, and Rafe wasn't at all interested in her.'

'But Amelia Good-bloody-body wasn't Rafe's first wife. The woman he fell in love with at first sight. The woman he married just a few weeks later. The woman who broke his heart. And not just in two. In thousands of tiny pieces. The woman who left him and who it took him most of his adult life to get over.'

'OK. I suppose I see your point. But did he welcome her with open arms, or was he cross that she'd turned up unannounced?'

'That's the worst part.'

'Wait. I thought you said the fact she was gorgeous was the worst part?'

'Oh for God's sake, Jo. Stop being so bloody pedantic, will you!'

'I would if I knew what it meant. Sorry. What's the other worst part? Tell me.'

'It's that, after he got over the initial shock of Carruthers telling him she was in the hall, he gave me the strangest look, dashed into his room and got dressed so fast I thought he was the one with super powers. Then he told me he'd be back and not to cut my feet on the glass.'

'You've lost me. What have super powers got to do with this? And why was he telling you not to cut your feet on the glass? What glass?'

'Why aren't you listening?'

'Why aren't you making any sense?'

'I am making sense. But I'm upset.'

'Well, I'm hungover.'

'I'm hungover too. But I've got to deal with this and I thought you might actually be some help.'

'OK. Sorry. That second worst part didn't sound too bad.'

'I hadn't actually got to the worst part. He left me standing there while he and Carruthers hurried towards the stairs.'

'Why didn't you go with him?'

'Will you please stop interrupting. I was only wearing a dressing gown and I know I must've looked a complete mess. But I did go and stand behind the massive newel post and the wooden gallery bit at the top of the staircase and looked down into the hall. That's how I know she's gorgeous. I couldn't see Rafe's face as he walked towards her but I could see hers.

She was smiling ecstatically. As if the world had just fallen into her lap. I heard him say, "Hello, Pippa. This is a surprise. What brings you to Wynter House?" As calmly as if she were a friend he hasn't seen for a while. And she said, "Hello, Rafe. I was going to call, but I was worried you might tell me not to come. And I wanted to see you." He didn't reply right away. And this is the worst part.'

'Dear God, Neva. How many worst parts are there?'

'Shut up. This one. This is the worst part. I leant forward so that I could hear better and from out of nowhere Cecil and Ronnie asked me what I was doing? They made me jump and I fell forward so I grabbed the newel post at the top of the stairs and I sort of swung around it. I managed to save myself from falling down the stairs, but I caught my foot in my dressing gown and ... well, let's just say that Pippa saw a side of me I'd really rather she hadn't.'

Jo laughed. She couldn't help herself. 'On my God, Neva. Front or back?'

'Back. Fortunately. But that was bad enough.'

'So basically, you swung on the newel post, a bit like a pole dancer would, and mooned your boyfriend's ex-wife? Good going, Neva. What did Rafe say about that?'

'I didn't wait to find out. I pulled myself upright, surprisingly with help from Cecil and

Ronnie, although they were definitely trying to stop themselves from laughing hysterically. I marched a few steps and then ran the rest of the way to Rafe's room and now I'm calling you. What should I do? Do I just sit here and wait and see if Rafe comes back? Or do I get showered and dressed and try to make myself look stunning and go downstairs and introduce myself as if nothing had happened?'

'Yeah right. Good luck with that. I hate to say this, Neva. But for once in my life, I have absolutely no idea what to tell you.'

'Perhaps if you stopped laughing like a demented hyena you might be able to think of something.'

Jo continued laughing although she did bite her lip for a second or two.

'Nope. Sorry. I've got nothing. All I can think about is the vision of you swinging around that ornate, oak newel post, baring your arse to Rafe's ex-wife.'

Chapter Eighteen

Neva heard a noise outside Rafe's bedroom door and raced over and opened it, half expecting Cecil and Ronnie to be there but hoping it was Rafe. Instead it was Carruthers and he was clearing up the mess of breakfast things on the floor.

'Oh. I'm sorry, Carruthers. I should've done that. But I was in a rush to phone my friend and ... You don't need to know about that. Here. Let me do it.'

'I wouldn't hear of it, Miss Neva. Taryn would usually deal with such things but she's helping Mrs Pyke. It seems everyone requires a late breakfast this morning.'

'Penny's making breakfast now?' Neva's stomach rumbled. 'Er. Is Rafe still with Pippa in the hall?'

He raised one brow and stood upright. 'No, Miss Neva.'

'She's gone?'

'No, Miss–'

'For God's sake, Carruthers. I thought we'd got past all that Miss Neva business. It's Neva. Just Neva.'

One brow shot up, but other than that he made no facial expressions, just gave her a slight bow.

'With Mrs Phyllida Wynter staying, I believe Mrs Olivia Wynter would prefer formality. I apologise, Miss Neva.'

'Wait. What? Did you just say Mrs Phyllida Wynter? And that she's staying?'

'Yes, Miss Neva.'

'But they're divorced. Pippa's not Mrs Wynter. She hasn't been for fourteen years.'

A brow went skyward. 'I believe, that although they did indeed, divorce, Mrs Phyllida Wynter retained the name of Wynter.'

'You have got to be joking.'

'No, Miss Neva.'

'And she's definitely staying? But just for the day?'

'For the weekend. Miss Thorn is preparing her room.'

'The weekend?' Neva clamped her hands over her mouth. She hadn't meant to shriek.

'I can take it from here, Archie. Thank you.' Rafe was striding towards them and he didn't look particularly happy.

'Yes, Mr Rafe. Shall I finish clearing this later?'

'Just leave it for now! Sorry, Archie. This

isn't your fault. Please forgive me.'

He placed a hand on the butler's arm as he drew near, and threw him a brief smile.

'Of course, Mr Rafe.' Carruthers gave a small bow and marched off down the hall.

Rafe turned and looked at Neva.

'We need to talk.'

'I don't like the sound of that. Why's Pippa here, Rafe?'

'I'd rather not discuss this in the hall. Shall we?'

He indicated they should go back into his room and Neva turned and walked inside, sitting on the end of the bed and pulling her dressing gown tightly around her.

'Well?' Neva hoped she didn't sound as nervous as she felt.

'What were you thinking, Neva? Standing in the hall with nothing on at such a time.'

'What? Really? That's what you're starting with? And you're annoyed about it? I was wearing a dressing gown! And I wasn't thinking. Not really. Hearing that my boyfriend's ex-wife had arrived and was waiting in the hall to see him clearly brought out the worst in me. It wasn't the joyful start to the morning I was expecting.'

'It wasn't a particularly joyful start to mine. But why didn't you just get dressed and come down and join us?'

'Because I didn't think you wanted me to.

You gave me the strangest look and then walked away saying you'd be back, and not to cut my feet on the glass. That kind of told me you wanted me to stay where I was.'

'Which you chose to ignore.'

'Ignore? I'm not a bloody pet dog, Rafe. You can't simply tell me to stay and expect me to do so. I wanted to see her. I wanted to hear what you said. And it seems you've said she can stay for the weekend! I don't know what to say. I thought this woman cheated on you, walked out on you and left you with a broken heart. I thought you hadn't heard from her in years. And she just turns up and you invite her to stay as if none of that had happened? And then you come up here and shout at Carruthers and tell me off! I thought you loved me, Rafe. I thought we were going to get married even though I wasn't actually proposing last night. I ...'

Oh God. Why had she said that last bit? Why had she said any of it? He looked angry, surprised and a little hurt, all at the same time.

'I do love you. You clearly have no idea how much. But what do you mean? You weren't actually proposing. Are you saying last night was a joke? A fake proposal? Because I took it seriously. I was actually flattered. I know we'd all had far too much to drink, but I thought you meant it.'

He glanced towards the signet ring she was twisting round and round on her finger.

'Oh God, I thought you had. No! What I mean is, I'm glad you did. I want to marry you. I just hadn't meant to propose. And certainly not last night. I wanted you to be the one to propose to me. But not yet. I was only asking if you thought you might ask me to marry you one day in the future. Only it didn't come out right. I mean ... I got swept up in what was going on and I ... Oh hell. I'm making a complete mess of this. None of that matters. What matters is you said yes and I'm so happy that you did.'

'Are you? Then why are we arguing?'

'Because you came up here and told me off! And because you've told your stunningly gorgeous ex-wife she can spend the weekend here. And because she still uses your surname, in spite of the fact you're divorced. And because ... because ... because I'm hungover, and I'm hungry, and ... I'm frightened.'

He had started to smile but it faded at the final word.

'Frightened? Of what? Of marrying me?'

'No! Of losing you, you idiot!'

He raised his brows. 'Losing me? Why would you be frightened of that? I thought I'd made it clear when you were worried about Amelia, that I love you and you're the only woman for me. Although calling me an idiot possibly isn't the best way to reassure me that you love me.' He walked towards her and crouched down, taking her hands in his. 'I'm sorry, Neva. This morning hasn't turned out at all as I had hoped. Yesterday was so wonderful and last night, when you proposed – or when I thought you had, I was the happiest man in the world. I shouldn't have got cross with you.' He laughed suddenly. 'I suppose your little exhibition just now was quite amusing. And understandable in a way. Pippa saw the funny side of it. And you do have a beautiful bottom.' He kissed her fingers and grinned at her.

'It's my best feature.'

He shook his head and grinned. 'It isn't. But I won't argue with you about it. I don't know what to say, except I'm sorry. Pippa coming here has ... I don't know... been somewhat disconcerting, to say the least. I honestly never expected to see her again and then there she was. She's hardly changed at all. The strange thing is, when she started talking, all the hurt and pain I thought would surge up, didn't. It was as if I were chatting to a friend. A friend I hadn't seen for a while.'

'But why is she here?'

'She's driven down from Oxford, which is where she now lives because she owns a couple of nightclubs. One in Oxford and one in London and she's heard about our gin – from other sources, not from me before you ask. She thinks it would be a great product to sell in her clubs. They're upmarket, exclusive, and cater mainly to the demographic at which we're aiming. From the brochure she briefly showed me, our gin does seem like a perfect fit.'

'That's great,' Neva said, when what she really meant was that's the worst news possible. Not only was his ex-wife successful, and no doubt rich from running two nightclubs, the woman had a legitimate reason to get in touch with Rafe.

'It is,' he agreed, smiling a bit too much for Neva's liking.

'But surely she could just order it online.'

'I suppose she could have done so, but she wanted to run a business proposal by me and before I knew it, I'd invited her to stay for breakfast. And then the day, so that we could discuss it with Sean and Adam. And then the weekend. She reminded me that she told me repeatedly, over eighteen years ago that I should get the gin distillery up and running again. But in those days, I was far too young and wet behind the ears, either to take that big a risk, or to incur Olivia's wrath by disobeying her commands.' He gave a little laugh and looked as if he were replaying memories in his head.

'Your ex-wife was the one who suggested it? And you're telling me I have no reason to be frightened?' Neva tried to hide the hurt she was feeling.

He looked surprised, as if he'd forgotten

she was there.

'Absolutely none. Pippa didn't make the suggestion. It was something I often talked about wanting to do. She merely told me to go for it. Probably at least once a month for a couple of years. But I was working in the City during the week, like Adam does now, and running the estate. There were so many other demands on my time regarding the house and grounds that I couldn't devote the hours or the energy it would require. Over the years, I thought about it several times, but it was only when Sean and I discussed becoming business partners that it really became a viable prospect. And yes, Pippa was my wife and yes, we have a history together. But it is history, Neva. As you said, Pippa cheated on me, left me and broke my heart. She's my past. You're my present. And my future. But does that mean that Pippa and I can't finally be friends?'

Neva met his gaze. He sounded sincere. He looked as if he were telling the truth. Yesterday had been the best day of her life. And they were now engaged. She'd been worried unnecessarily about Amelia. Perhaps she was worrying unnecessarily about Pippa.

'I don't know. I'm not sure.'

'Don't you trust me?'

'Yes. I trust you completely. It's Pippa I have doubts about.'

He grinned and kissed her on the forehead.

'Come and meet her and then you can see for yourself.' He stood up, still holding her hands in his and eased her to her feet. 'I think you'll like her. But maybe get dressed first.' He laughed and kissed her briefly on the mouth before turning away and heading towards the door. 'We'll be in the dining room. Penny's making breakfast. It seems several of us got up late today.' He winked at her as he closed the door behind him.

Neva didn't want to like Pippa bloody Wynter. She wanted her to go away.

She definitely wasn't looking forward to meeting her. Especially after mooning her. Should she apologise? What would Olivia Wynter do? Well, obviously Olivia wouldn't get herself into such a ridiculous situation, but if she ever did, she would probably just behave as if it hadn't happened. That's what Neva would do.

She showered quickly and searched through the few clothes she had in Rafe's wardrobe, cursing because they were either very dressy and formal, or very casual, like jeans and jumpers. She only had one ordinary dress in there and that was rather plain. In the end, she decided not to try too hard. Pippa would notice that. Neva would wear jeans and a jumper and show the woman that she didn't need to dress up for Rafe to love her. Which was actually true. She didn't. Rafe genuinely seemed to love her just the way she was.

And now, if she had really understood correctly, she and Rafe were engaged. He had taken her proposal as just that. A genuine proposal. And he'd said yes. Would he mention that to Pippa? Would he announce it to everyone at breakfast? Should she say anything about it? No. She would just wave her hand around a lot and hope that someone would notice she was wearing Rafe's signet ring on the third finger of her left hand. Surely Judith might? Or even Hazel? Or possibly Adam? Cecil and Ronnie would say something if they spotted it. She would have to hope they hadn't had breakfast when they'd saved her from a fall earlier.

She opened the bedroom door and noticed the smashed items had now all been cleared away. She hurried along the hall and down the stairs, stopping just before the dining room door and taking a couple of soothing deep breaths. She could hear laughter from inside. A woman's laugh. A light, cheery and rather sexy laugh. And Rafe's laugh. A hearty, happy laugh. And Adam and Hazel. Even Ethel was cackling away. Everyone sounded very jolly and as she walked into the room, smiling and holding her head high, no one even noticed her.

Rafe was sitting at the head of the long table as he usually did and Pippa sat to his right – the seat where Neva usually sat. Adam sat opposite with Hazel beside him, and Wendy, Sean and Taryn next to her, along with Penny and her husband, Roger. Judith was seated next to Pippa, with Gavin by her side. George, Ethel, Queenie, Cecil and Ronnie also sat at that side of the table. All the chairs were occupied other than some seats further along.

It was bad enough that Pippa was sitting in Neva's place, and that Rafe hadn't saved her a seat, but what made it even worse was that he and Pippa were looking at one another and laughing in a way that sent a hundred knives and forks into Neva's heart.

Chapter Nineteen

Neva tried to decide what to do.

Should she quietly walk to a vacant chair and sit down or should she go up to Rafe, kiss him on the cheek and say a loud and falsely cheerful, 'Good morning' to everybody?

'You're dressed then?' Ethel said, rather loudly, as Neva dithered.

All heads turned towards Neva and it was as if they all fell silent. Except they didn't. Not really. It just felt as if they had. She spotted Cecil and Ronnie, nodding and giggling. They'd no doubt spread the news of Neva's embarrassment. Was that what everyone had been laughing so loudly about?

'Yes, Ethel,' Neva said, feigning an air of confidence she didn't feel. 'Although I did consider coming down in my dressing gown. I do like to make an entrance.'

She had no idea what she was waffling about. Nerves were getting the better of her. She forced a smile for Ethel and walked towards an empty seat but Rafe called to her.

'Neva. Come and meet Pippa.'

He got up and went to her, taking her hand and leading her towards the table. He grabbed another chair on the way from a row along one wall and deftly put it beside his, moving his over so that they could sit side by side at the head of the table.

Pippa stood up and held out her hand saying, 'Hi. I'm Pippa. It's lovely to meet you.' Her smile looked friendly and sincere.

Neva took Pippa's hand and shook it. 'Hi. I'm Neva. Rafe's ... girlfriend.'

Why had she hesitated? Why had she added the bit about being his girlfriend? It sounded as if she were staking her claim. And why hadn't she said his fiancée, if she was going to be such a complete and utter moron?

Rafe gave her a sideways glance with a questioning look in his eyes. Perhaps he was wondering the same thing.

The smile on Pippa's perfect mouth faded suddenly, but a second later it was back, although she didn't look quite as happy as before.

She darted a look at Rafe. 'I didn't realise you were seeing someone. Perhaps it's best if I don't stay.'

'Why? It's not a problem.' Rafe glanced from Neva to Pippa and back to Neva. 'Is it, Neva?'

Yes, it damn well is, Neva wanted to say. Instead she smiled and shook her head as she sat down, saying, 'No. No problem at all.'

Rafe resumed his seat and wrapped an arm around her. That at least made her feel a little reassured.

Pippa lowered her head slightly. 'I should've called. I don't know what I was thinking.'

Rafe gave Neva another strange look. 'There seems to be a lot of that going around.' He smiled at Pippa. 'You're here now. Don't worry about it. Let's enjoy breakfast and you can tell us more about your clubs. Oh. But first, I believe I have an announcement to make.' He got to his feet and nodded at Adam.

'I'll get the champagne.' Adam jumped up, smiling and dashed to the large, ornate silver, champagne trug sitting on the oak sideboard, beside which Carruthers now stood, holding a tray of empty glasses.

Neva gave a tiny gasp and stared adoringly at Rafe. He was going to announce their engagement!

Instead he smiled at Judith and Gavin who beamed at him and at one another.

Hazel, Penny and Taryn joined Adam and started handing round glasses of champagne.

'Last night,' Rafe said, 'and I have to be honest and say, much to my surprise and I think even to his and his beautiful fiancée's too,

Judith and Gavin got engaged. They're going to marry in our chapel, right here in this house.'

Almost everyone looked astonished, apart from those who had witnessed it last night. And George and Ethel it seemed.

'I told you, Queenie,' Ethel said, holding out her hand. 'Pay up.' Then she beamed, toothlessly at Judith and Gavin. 'Congratulations. It took you long enough to tell her, Gavin. I thought I'd be dead and buried before you finally did. I was tempted to tell her myself.'

'You knew I loved Judith?' Gavin laughed as he pulled Judith into his arms. 'I thought George was the only one who knew.'

'I didn't say a word,' George said.

Ethel cackled. 'The puppy-dog way you look at her was a bit of a clue. I know you do your best to hide it, but I see everything.'

Cecil and Ronnie's mouths both formed perfect 'O's.

'We never saw that,' Cecil said.

Ronnie shook his head. 'We didn't suspect a thing!'

'You kept that close to your chest,' Sean said, grinning. 'I had no idea.'

Rafe tapped his glass with a spoon and laughed. 'Nor did I. And we've been friends for years.'

Judith laughed. 'The foolish man thought I was a little in love with both you and Adam, which is why he wouldn't tell you.'

She gave Gavin a playful slap and then kissed him full on the mouth and everyone cheered.

Rafe and Adam both looked taken aback, but they smiled and shrugged.

Rafe continued,'We can debate the whys and wherefores later. For now, let's just toast the happy couple. I know you'll all join me in congratulating them both and wishing them a long, happy and prosperous future together.'

Now that everyone had champagne, all glasses were raised and Judith and Gavin's health and happiness was toasted.

Neva raised her glass, along with everyone else, but she stuffed her left hand into the pocket of her jeans. And she kept it hidden all through breakfast, which was no easy feat. She had to drink and eat using only her right hand and Rafe gave her very curious looks more than once throughout.

But the only engagement he had mentioned was Judith and Gavin's. If anyone spotted his signet ring on Neva's wedding finger, they would be bound to comment. Perhaps Rafe wanted this morning to be about Judith and Gavin and that was why he had kept silent about him and Neva.

Or perhaps now, he *was actually* having second thoughts.

Chapter Twenty

Jo wasn't just surprised; she was a little annoyed. She loved Neva to bits but sometimes the girl was so wrapped up in herself and her problems that she completely forgot about everyone else and theirs.

'And you're only telling me about Gavin and Judith now? You didn't think to mention it when you called me earlier this morning? Thanks a lot for nothing.'

Neva's gasp at the other end of the phone line was audible.

'I'm so sorry, Jo. I really am. I've been so caught up in my own web of problems. Are you upset? Shall I come back to the flat? I will if you want me to, despite being terrified to leave Rafe alone with Pippa for even a second. Sorry again. That sounded as if I'm trying to guilt you into saying you don't need me there. I'm not. I'm happy to come back, if you want.'

'Oh do shut up.' Jo let out a long sigh. 'I'm not upset. Just disappointed. But I knew Gavin wasn't interested in me, so it's no great loss, is it? And as it happens, I have some news myself. But let's sort this out first. So you're saying Rafe told you that he had taken your proposal as genuine and as far as he was concerned, you're engaged, but then he didn't announce your engagement when he announced Judith and Gavin's and now you're not sure if you're engaged or not. Is that the long and the short of it?'

'Yes. But what's your news? Is it anything exciting? Have you met someone new?'

Jo tutted. 'Yeah right. I was still in bed when you called me at 10 and I'm still in bed now, even though it's almost lunchtime. Where, exactly, would I have met someone new?'

'Sorry. You said you had news and I thought ... OK. What's the news then?'

'Rob called me just before you did. He's going to be coming down here tomorrow and he wondered if I might be free to meet up! You know what that means, don't you? It means Hazel's brilliant text worked. Rob is jealous and he's been thinking about it since last Sunday and now he's going out of his way to come down here to see me. I'm going to be having sex tomorrow! Yay! Oh, so whatever happens with you and Rafe I need you to stay at Wynter House all day on Sunday, right? Neva? Did you hear me?'

'Yes. Yes, I heard you. That's fantastic. I suppose.'

'Try not to give yourself a hernia with all the jubilation you feel for me.'

'I'm sorry, Jo. I am happy for you. Really happy. If that's what you want. But didn't he say he was seeing someone else now?'

'Yeah. And?'

'So you're saying you'll have sex with him, regardless of that?'

'OK, I know it's wrong, but we were together for four whole years and we were engaged. They've just started dating. Rob and I have history. What's a bit of sex between old friends?'

'God. I hope Rafe and Pippa don't think like you. Because if they had sex and I found out, I'd shove them both over Wyntersleap Falls.'

'Rafe's not going to have sex with Pippa. Not after all these years. But even if he did, it's just sex, Neva. It's not a marriage proposal. And talking of marriage proposals, which was why you called. In answer to your question, no. I don't think you should ask Rafe why he didn't announce your engagement. You didn't say you were his fiancée when you introduced yourself, did you? You said you were his girlfriend. Perhaps he's thinking you're the one who doesn't want your engagement announced. My advice is, say nothing until you're in bed tonight and then just try and discuss it rationally and reasonably. It's really cold today so you can wear gloves so that no one will see the signet ring. Or you could just take it off and say you're terrified of losing it and you think it's best if he has it back until you do make it official. I sincerely hope he's going to get you a proper engagement ring anyway.'

'Firstly, Jo, it is never "just sex". At least not as far as I'm concerned. Secondly, you've now given me something else to worry about, so thanks for that. Perhaps he does think I'm the one having second thoughts. But I do like your suggestion. The one about me saying I don't want to lose the ring. Not the one about wearing gloves. That's just silly. I can't walk around the house wearing gloves.'

'Carruthers does.'

Neva tutted. 'He's the butler. And he only does that if Olivia makes him. No. I'll give Rafe back his ring and say that stuff you said. But I'll do it before tonight just in case anyone sees it. And I need to tell him why I've done it because if he spots that it's not there, then he really might get confused about what's going on.'

'He won't be the only one! I'm confused. Why is your love life so complicated?'

'Says the girl who is about to have sex with her ex-fiancé, who she couldn't wait to get away from only a few short weeks ago and who is now dating someone else, and who thinks she's dating the owner of a stately home.'

'Bugger off.' Jo laughed down the phone. 'I love you, you nutter. But I've just realised I'm starving and I really fancy fish and chips. I'm going to hang up, make myself look stunning and go and practise some, in this case harmless, flirting with Ed. And just so that you know. Ed is Ed Fisher, who owns The Perfect Plaice, the fish shop which I thought his dad owned and who is married to a buxom blonde with a voice like fingernails being dragged down a chalkboard, and whose nose I broke a week ago. Ed's. Not his wife's. We had a bit of banter and I'm sure he won't mind one bit.'

'His wife might mind.'

'I'll explain it's for a good cause. I'll tell her I need to have sex.'

This time Neva laughed. 'I'd love to hear what she has to say about that.'

'I'll tell you later when you'll, no doubt, be calling to give me an update on your on-off engagement and the battle with Rafe's ex-wife.'

Jo hung up and leapt out of bed, her hangover gone and feeling happier than she'd expected. OK, Gavin was engaged, but at least she had the prospect of some sex to look forward to. And sooner than she had expected. She was having a tiny pang of guilt about Rob's new girlfriend, but they had only recently started dating and they may not be exclusive.

She'd worry about that tomorrow. All she

wanted now was food.

She was showered, dressed and had applied just the right amount of make-up, all in less than thirty minutes. She wrapped up warm; it was definitely chilly today. The heating had gone off at 9 and she'd had to get up and switch it on to 'all day'.

She hurried to The Perfect Plaice and this time, opened the door more carefully. Ed was behind the counter, frying fish and chips and when he looked up, he sort of did a double take. Then he smiled and it was as if the temperature had shot up by several degrees.

'Hello, Jo. This is a lovely surprise. I see your eye's healed. And you're looking quite a bit different from the way you looked last week. Have you come to break my heart this time?'

Heat rushed through her, and it wasn't entirely due to the warmth from the fryers.

'Hello, Ed. So are you. Your nose is fixed I see. Where did you get that tan? Or is it make-up?'

He grinned at her and met her gaze from under long, dark lashes.

'It's from a bottle. And the plastic surgeon is sending you the bill for my nose.'

'You should've asked him to do some other work while you were there.'

'I did. But he said I was a perfect specimen and if anyone tells me different I should send them to an optician.'

Jo grinned at him. 'I didn't see you at the Merriment Bay Moonlight Valentine's Dance, which was surprising given you were desecrating your door with a sign promoting it.'

He raised his head and looked her directly in the eye.

'You looked for me?'

Jo blushed from head to toe.

'Only so that I could show my friend my handiwork. Your nose, like men's hearts, isn't the only one I've broken.'

'I can believe that.' He grinned again. 'But you did look for me?'

'Only because the men in my age group numbered about five, and most of those are dating my friends.'

The grin turned into a smile. 'You don't have a boyfriend?'

'Er ... As it happens, I've just got out of a long relationship and a short engagement. But I'm seeing my ex tomorrow. He's coming here all the way from Upminster.'

'What for? Are you getting back together?'

'No. That's not the plan.'

'So why are you seeing him? Is it to get back your stuff?'

'My stuff? If you mean my expensive and tasteful clothes, personal possessions, and such, then no. I got those back before I moved down here?'

'Why then?'

'Is it really any of your business?' Jo laughed.

'It could be.'

She hesitated. He was flirting and she was enjoying it. But he was married.

'I'm seeing him because ... we're friends.'

'You mean because you're missing him?' He tossed a bowl of raw chips into the fryer.

'No. I miss the sex.'

His head shot up and he grinned.

'You don't have to see your ex to have sex. I know someone who could help you out with that.'

'I bet you do. But your wife might have something to say about it.'

'My wife?'

'Don't look so surprised. And please don't give me the usual line.'

'Er. I don't have a wife, so I don't know what the usual line is.'

'Oh come on, Ed. I like you, so please don't try to lie to me. I saw her. She was here the day we met.'

'My wife?' he repeated. 'I honestly don't know ... oh bloody hell. You mean the beautiful, buxom woman who was tending tables and strangling what was probably once a lovely tune?'

'Yes.'

He burst out laughing before pulling a face. 'That wasn't my wife. That was my mum! Well my step-mum, but as she's the only mum I've known, I call her Mum.'

'Your mum?' Jo couldn't believe it. 'But she kissed you on the cheek and called you baby and our banter ended and you clammed up tighter than a politician caught with his pants down the minute she came in.'

He nodded. 'Nice analogy. That was because she's always trying to fix me up and if she'd realised I was interested in you, she would've dragged you through to the back and started showing you baby photos of me, whilst planning our wedding. I love her. I honestly do. She's got a heart of gold and she adores me and my dad. Only not in the same way, you understand. But the woman drives me nuts sometimes. I didn't want to ruin my chances.'

He held her gaze for a moment before looking down at the fryers and shaking a wire basket filled with heavenly smelling chips.

'Ruin your chances?' Jo queried. 'OK. Two questions. No. Make that three.'

'Fire away.'

'One. Did you just say you were interested in me when we met? Even though I was covered in paint and looked a mess?'

'Yes. But you didn't look a mess. You looked lovely.'

Jo gave him a tiny smile. 'Two. Then why didn't you come to the salon during the following week to try to see me again or to ask me out? And why weren't you at the Merriment Bay Moonlight Valentine's Dance to see if I was there?'

'Is that two questions, or one?'

'One. Split into two parts. Answer please.'

'OK. I noticed you weren't wearing a ring but I didn't know if you had a boyfriend. The day after we met, I was going away on a friend's stag do and wedding. So thanks again for the broken nose. It looked great in all the photos.' He winked and grinned. 'Four nights in Ibiza with all my rugby mates. Don't judge. Followed by three days at some snazzy hotel in the posh part of Majorca. I only got back last night.'

'Wow! That raises a whole host of other questions, but it actually answers my third one.'

'Which was?'

'Whether that tan was really from a bottle. Because if it was, I'd have to say, forget it right now. There's no way I'd consider dating a man who wears fake tan. Unless he were a sexy dancer on *Strictly*. Or an actor.'

'Thanks for the heads up. Now I've got a question? Three, in fact.'

Jo grinned. 'Fire away.'

He leant his strong-looking forearms on the counter, bent one arm up and raised one finger.

'One. Does that mean you'd consider dating me?'

Jo tipped her head to one side. 'Possibly.'

'I need a definite answer, please.'

'Yes.'

He grinned and raised a second finger. 'Two. If I asked you out, would you cancel your booty call with your ex? Because I think I might have a bit of an issue with that.'

Jo raised her brows. 'It's been a while since I've had sex. I'm getting pretty desperate. But if you asked me out fairly soon, I might.'

He grinned again and slapped his palm down on the counter.

'OK. Three. What do you want?'

'Want? Are we talking about sex?'

He laughed. 'We can. I'd quite like to. But what I actually meant was, what do you want to eat? Huss and chips again, or something different?'

She burst out laughing. 'Huss and chips, please. And this time, I'm going to eat in.'

'Huss and chips coming up.' He turned to get a plate from a shelf to his right and threw her a sideways grin. 'If I pay for them and sit and have a sandwich with you, could we class this as our first date? After all, this is The Perfect Plaice.'

'Funny. I suppose we could. But why?'

'It's just that you seem to be in a bit of a rush to get to the sex bit. Not that I'm complaining, believe me. But I make it a rule not to have sex with anyone until we've been on at least three dates.'

Jo laughed but forced herself to be serious. 'Really? Well in that case, you gave me my fish and chips free last week, and we did have bodily contact, so perhaps we should count that as date number one and this as date number two.'

'I like the sound of that. What are you doing tonight? I should be working but if I tell my mum I've got a date, she'll be happy for her and my dad to come and hold the fort. And that'll be date number three.'

'Then I suggest you call your mum.'

He beamed at her. 'And will you call your ex? Or are you going to wait and see how dates number two and three go first?'

Jo licked her bottom lip provocatively. 'No. I'll call him this afternoon. I have a feeling dates number two and three will go very well indeed. And I'm already looking forward to date number four.'

'So am I. What are you doing on Sunday?'

Jo leant on the counter. 'Unless I'm mistaken, pretty much the same as I was planning to do. Only with you instead of my ex. And I think I'm going to enjoy it a whole lot more.'

'Fantastic. No pressure then. Your place or mine?'

'Yours. After all, this is The Perfect Plaice.'

Chapter Twenty-One

Neva was looking for Rafe. After speaking with Jo she had decided what to do. She'd give him back his ring and say she was worried she might lose it. She'd also say that what with Judith and Gavin's engagement, and now Pippa staying the weekend, she didn't want anyone asking questions about why she was wearing it. He wasn't upstairs, and he wasn't in the distillery. Only Sean and Adam were there.

Carruthers was marching across the hall but he stopped and smiled at Neva.

'Ah, Carruthers. Have you seen Rafe?'

He hesitated for a second and his brow rose slower than usual.

'I believe he may be in his study, Miss ...' He gave a small cough. 'I mean, Neva.'

Neva grinned at him. 'Thank you, Carruthers. On both counts.' She turned towards Rafe's study.

'M ... Neva. I believe Mrs Phyllida Wynter may be with him.'

Neva wasn't sure if that were merely a statement or a warning for her to be prepared, but she was grateful in either event and thanked him again.

The door to the study was ajar and yet Neva couldn't hear voices. Irrational panic set in and she shoved the door open without knocking. The room looked empty until Pippa swung the large, leather high-backed chair around. Rafe's chair. Pippa was sitting in Rafe's chair – and she looked very much at home.

Pippa smiled. 'Hello again. I was admiring the view. I'd forgotten how beautiful it was from this room.'

Neva stiffened. 'It's beautiful from every room. Especially Rafe's bedroom.' What a stupid thing to say. Even Neva cringed.

Pippa, on the other hand, merely grinned. 'Yes. Although I didn't spend much time looking out of that particular window.'

The cow! Was she saying that she and Rafe were far too busy doing other things to look out of his bloody window?

Pippa continued: 'Rafe tells me you're a hairdresser and you're opening your own salon in Merriment Bay.'

Did he also tell you we're engaged? Neva wanted to say. Instead she nodded like an idiot.

'How wonderful,' Pippa went on. 'I can never do anything with my hair. It's always such a mess. Perhaps you could do something with it?'

Like cut off every beautiful inch of it. Neva stared at Pippa, whose long golden tresses were the image of perfection, although clearly not her natural colour. What was that? Had Rafe ever mentioned it? There were no photos of Pippa in the house... Thank God.

Neva cleared her throat. 'I'm sure I could do something with it. Sadly, the salon isn't open yet. My best friend and I are currently refurbishing the place.'

'How exciting. I remember doing that with the first nightclub I opened. There's nothing quite like that feeling of pride and achievement when you open the doors for the first time when it's finished. Is there much to do?'

'Not really. We're just taking our time because we want it to be perfect. Rafe's sister and niece have just painted the most beautiful trompe l'oeil on one of the walls. It exceeded all our expectations, but then Cat and Kyra are extremely talented artists, so we knew it would be wonderful.'

'Rafe's sister and niece?' Pippa was giving her the strangest look.

'Yes. Cat and ...' Oh God. Rafe hadn't told her about them yet. That made Neva smile, even though it shouldn't. 'Er. He hasn't told you about Cat and Kyra, has he?'

'No. He hasn't. But then we haven't really had that much time to talk. So Phillip had an affair, did he? And that produced a child. Hmm. I have to say, I'm not entirely surprised.'

She seemed to be taking the news as if she'd just been told Rafe had a new car.

'And it's really a private, family matter,' Neva said. She could be bitchy too.

'That put me in my place. You don't want me here, do you, Neva?'

The comment took Neva by surprise. 'Er. It really doesn't matter to me. And you're only staying for the weekend.'

Pippa rested her elbows on the arms of Rafe's chair and put the tips of her fingers together, a bit like a church steeple.

'Am I?'

Neva definitely didn't like the expression on Pippa's gorgeous face.

'That's what Rafe told me.' Neva held her head high and stuck out her chin. 'Carruthers told me he was here, but I see he isn't, so I'll see you later.'

'He's with Olivia. She sent him a summons via Judith. He shouldn't be long. You're welcome to wait.'

Welcome to wait! Who the hell did she think she was?

'Thanks. But I've got things I need to be getting on with.'

'We could be friends, I think. In different circumstances. And I really don't want to hurt you.'

Neva had turned to leave but she stopped and swivelled back round to face Pippa.

'Hurt me? Is that some sort of threat?' Neva snorted with derision, although she was a tiny bit intimidated. Pippa owned nightclubs. Perhaps she was one of those female Mafia bosses Neva and Jo liked reading about in novels. Did such women exist in real life? Was Pippa one of them?

'No. What I meant was, I didn't know you existed when I came here. If I had, I might not have come. Although you and Rafe haven't been dating long, from what I hear. Not that that means anything. Rafe and I only dated for a matter of weeks before he proposed.'

'Why have you come? I mean, really. Was it just to do a deal on Wyntersleap Gin? Or was there another reason?'

'I think you know the answer to that, Neva. But I'll be honest, because I like you. I meant it when I said we could be friends in different circumstances. I truly think we could. But clearly, here and now, we can't. Because we both want the same thing. We both want Rafe.'

Neva gasped. She hadn't expected such honesty, especially as there wasn't a shred of bitchiness in Pippa's tone. She actually sounded sad. As if she regretted the situation.

'So I was right. But the thing is, Pippa, Rafe is with me. You had your chance and you blew it. Within three years of being married, you'd cheated on him. Then you left him and broke his heart. Other than five years later, when you sent him divorce papers, which he told me he gladly signed, you haven't been in touch even once.'

Pippa didn't answer right away. She simply stared at Neva. After a few seconds she let out a long sorrowful sigh.

'You're right. What can I say? I was young. I was foolish. I was in love.'

Neva sucked in a breath. Those were almost the exact words Rafe had used when he'd explained why he married Pippa.

'Rafe told me he doesn't think you ever really loved him. You married him because you thought he had money.'

Now it was Pippa who gasped. 'Rafe told you that?'

Neva nodded and Pippa slumped back into the padded chair and shook her head repeatedly.

'Are you denying it?'

'Yes. And I don't think Rafe believes that either. I think it's just a defence.'

'A defence? For what?'

'Do you get on with Olivia, Neva?'

'What? What has Olivia got to do with this?'

'Everything. Please answer the question. And honestly.'

Neva coughed. 'I've only met her once or

twice. She keeps to her rooms most of the time.'

'You're not telling me the truth. Or at least, not the whole truth, are you?'

There was something about Pippa that made Neva want to tell her. Perhaps the bloody woman was right. Perhaps they could have been friends ... in different circumstances.

'Fine. I can't stand her and she despises me. She thinks, because I'm a hairdresser, I'm not good enough for Rafe.'

Pippa smiled and nodded. 'Thank you for that. She's old now, but nineteen years ago, when I first came to Wynter House, Olivia was still very much in charge. I was a barmaid when Rafe met and married me. Olivia refused to come to our wedding. When I arrived, she treated me as if I were an unpleasant smell. One that she could get rid of if she worked on it. And believe me, she did work on it. She constantly undermined me. If I asked any of the staff, and there were more staff in those days, to do something, Olivia told them not to. And they always obeyed Olivia. Ask Ethel and Queenie. They were both still working here then. Although Ethel retired before I finally left. Anyway, Olivia made my life hell.'

Neva could believe that. Olivia was intimidating even though she rarely came down, Neva could imagine how terrifying the woman must have been when she could march around the house giving orders.

'But you were Rafe's wife. Didn't he speak to Olivia?'

Pippa shook her head. 'Rafe was twenty when we married. We moved here to live as soon as he left uni. And he worked in the City during the week. Long hours, so even when I joined him in London, I was on my own most of the time. And Rafe wanted me here. He wanted me to 'run' the house.' Pippa let out a strangled laugh. 'Me! Run this house? Olivia wouldn't hear of it. She told Rafe I wasn't up to it. That I didn't understand the way of things. She was right about that. I didn't have a clue.'

'But surely Rafe understood that?' Neva was beginning to feel a teensy bit sorry for the nineteen-year-old Pippa. And yet, oddly jealous.

'Yes and no. He told me I should, "Let Olivia show you how things are done". I tried to tell him that she hated me, but he said I was imagining it. That she was firm but fair. That she found it hard to show her feelings. Believe me, she had no trouble showing her feelings when Rafe wasn't looking. But she was sweetness and light when he was around. Still firm, but wise and understanding. It was as if she were two completely different people.'

'Didn't he believe you?'

She shrugged. 'I believe he tried to. But he seemed to think I was just in awe of Olivia and the house. That I couldn't cope with the responsibility. And Rafe had so many other things to think about. We had no money. Letters were arriving from the banks every week, threatening action if the loan repayments weren't met. The staff were all old and about to retire. The house was falling down around his ears. In a way, I was just another burden. A chain around his neck. I'm not saying he felt that, but I did. We hardly spent any time together and when we did, he was always knackered. I was young, I was vibrant. I had dreams. When I married him, I was head over heels in love. I had visions of a fairy tale life at Wynter House. Of parties, and weekend guests. You know. All the stuff you see on TV. But what I stepped into was a nightmare. I'm not blaming Rafe. He told me he didn't have money. He said the house needed constant repairs. But I was wearing rose tinted glasses.'

'And they came off when you got here?'

Pippa shook her head again and smiled wanly. 'No. Not at first. But after a few months, they didn't just come off, they smashed into tiny pieces. I loved Rafe. I really did. But I was lonely. I was way out of my depth. I had no friends down here. No job. Nothing. Rafe had dreams. He wanted to get the distillery up and running but he was too concerned about the financial risk and about upsetting Olivia. She had decreed – and I do mean, decreed, that the Old Barn was out of bounds and the doors would never be re-opened. In those days, Rafe would never go behind Olivia's back. Her word was law. I kept telling him to do it. I had all sorts of plans for the place, but he just kept mothballing them. We spent even less time together, not that Rafe seemed to notice. I honestly think he thought we were fine. I grew lonelier and more depressed. I wanted to have a child, to start a family, but Rafe said we'd need to wait.'

'A child? Of course you did. I'm sorry. I don't know why I said that.'

'Rafe's reaction was the same when I told him.' Pippa laughed, but it wasn't the happy, sensual laugh of earlier. 'He said we had plenty of time to start a family. What he needed to do was get the house on a sound financial footing. Not what *we* needed to do. What *he* needed to do. And that was part of the problem. Even he excluded me and he didn't even know he was doing it.'

'Is that all true?'

Rafe's strangled tones made both Neva and Pippa jump. They stared at him and at one another.

'How long have you been there?' Pippa asked.

'Long enough to hear things I had no idea about. Is all that true, Pippa?'

'It's not like you to eavesdrop?' Pippa glared at him.

'I apologise. I heard you talking and I heard Neva's voice too. I was hoping you'd get to know one another and I was about to leave you to it when I heard what you said about Olivia treating you badly and undermining you with the staff.'

'Oh my God, Rafe! You heard all of it.' Pippa looked genuinely upset as she jumped up from his chair.

'Yes. And I wish I'd heard it all a long, long time ago.'

'I tried to tell you, but you didn't seem to take it in.'

'You should've made me listen.'

'Would it have made any difference?'

'It might have.'

Neva didn't like the way this conversation was going.

'Why didn't you try to talk to him? Why did you have an affair?'

Rafe and Pippa looked at Neva as if they'd forgotten she was there. Rafe furrowed his brows and fixed his gaze on Pippa.

She didn't answer right away and the tension in the air was palpable but Pippa finally sucked in a breath and pushed her shoulders back.

'Because I was lonely. You didn't seem to want me, Rafe, or notice me, or even speak to me half the time. All you seemed to care about was this house. It consumed you, night and day. Adam was there and he understood. Partly because you treated him in the same way.'

Silence fell between them but their eyes spoke volumes.

'Adam?' Neva said, her voice slightly hoarse from holding back her emotions. 'What has Adam got to do with your affair?'

Rafe glanced at her and shook his head. 'It was years ago. It doesn't matter.'

Realisation dawned.

'Oh my God! Pippa and Adam had an affair!'

Rafe had never told Neva who Pippa had had the affair with. No wonder he had been so jealous when he thought Neva had fancied Adam. And yet he'd never, ever mentioned Adam and Pippa's affair. And nor had Adam. They'd both behaved as if it had been some unnamed man.

Rafe had obviously forgiven Adam. But had he forgiven Pippa? He'd told Neva Pippa was dead to him. Did he blame her for the affair? Did he think she had seduced his younger brother, possibly to hurt Rafe even more?

Pippa glanced at Neva. 'I'm not proud of it.'

'You seemed to be at the time,' Rafe said, a hint of bitterness creeping back into his voice as he maintained eye contact with his ex-wife. 'You threw it in my face – along with your engagement and wedding rings, I seem to recall.'

'I was angry. I was heartbroken. I think, perhaps, I actually hated you at that precise moment.'

'Double that, and you may have some idea how I felt at the time.'

'I was trying to get you to react. I wanted you to say you loved me and you understood. I wanted you to take me in your arms and say you'd forgive me and everything would be OK.'

'Is that what you wanted? I had no idea. And if so, I'm not sure you went about it the right way. What I remember is you giving me an ultimatum. Telling me to choose between you and Wynter House. Insisting that we move away and start our lives somewhere else. And when I said I couldn't possibly leave here, you screamed that I could have the sodding house and the sodding family heirlooms and my sodding brother. But that I should know that you'd had enough of me, of this mausoleum, of that bitch, Olivia, and even of sleeping with Adam. Or have I misremembered any of that?'

Neva gasped and Rafe shot another momentary glance in her direction but his attention quickly reverted to Pippa, who shook her head and lowered her eyes with a heavy sigh as if the world had tumbled down around her.

'No. I think you've remembered it almost word for word. Isn't it strange how we can both remember the worst day of our lives, almost word perfect, and yet we probably can't do so for all the good ones? And there were good ones, weren't there, Rafe? Some very good ones.'

He let out a sigh and Neva noticed the tension in his entire body seemed to drift away as he slowly smiled at Pippa.

'Yes, Pippa. Yes, there were.'

Neva looked from Rafe to Pippa and back again.

Then she hung her head so that neither of them could see the tears she was fighting back and she hurried from the room.

Chapter Twenty-Two

Rafe knew he should go after Neva. She hadn't exactly stormed out and she hadn't shouted or screamed or even said a word, but she was probably upset by what she had just heard. He was upset and he had been a party to it all. Although he clearly hadn't understood any of what had really happened all those years ago. And he needed to. Perhaps, in any case, Neva would prefer some time on her own to let it all sink in. It didn't really change anything for her. But Pippa's words had changed a great deal for him.

'You were honestly telling the truth?' he asked, meeting Pippa's eyes.

She held her right hand in the air and smiled sheepishly.

'Yes. The truth, the whole truth, nothing but the truth. I swear.'

He could see that she was.

'I didn't know half of the things you said. I sound like a complete idiot. A blind fool. Was I really that bad?'

'Yes.' She gave a little laugh. 'You were. I'm not blaming you though, Rafe. Truly I'm not. I should've stood up to Olivia. I should've fought for what I wanted. And I should never, ever have slept with Adam.' She gave a little shrug.

'That last part I definitely agree with.' He forced a smile. 'I forgave him fairly quickly. He was only eighteen at the time.' He shook his head. 'And you were irresistible in those days.'

Pippa raised her perfect brows. 'In those days? You mean I'm not irresistible now?'

He scanned her from head to toe without meaning to and gave a cough when he realised he was.

'You haven't changed.'

'That's good to hear. You thought I seduced him, didn't you? That I slept with him just to hurt you. I didn't, you know. It just sort of happened. We were both feeling a bit left out. Both craving your attention. He idolised you back then. I think he still does. And Olivia terrified him in those days almost as much as she terrified me. We grew closer together the further you seemed to push the two of us away from you. He was about to go off to uni and I think he was missing you and Wynter House even before he had to leave. I knew I couldn't go on the way things were for very much longer. But I loved you so much, Rafe. I know you'll find that hard to believe, but I did. I think, perhaps, part of me knew that the only way I would ever be able to leave you was if I did something terrible. If I did something it would take you years to forgive. So I kissed Adam and he kissed me back and before we knew it. Well, I don't have to join the dots.'

'Please don't. I did that enough times myself.'

'The minute it was over we both knew it had been a terrible mistake. I regretted it with every fibre of my being, and I know he did too. We agreed that you must never know and we tried to carry on as if it hadn't happened. But Olivia knew. God knows how but she did. And she told me that if I didn't tell you, she would, although she felt it should come from me. But my heart was breaking, Rafe. So I gave you the ultimatum. I think I knew even then what you would say. But part of me hoped it wasn't too late. I was sure you loved me, deep down.'

'Deep down? God, Pippa, I loved you more than I'd ever loved anyone or anything.'

She shook her head. 'You say that – and I do believe you think you mean it. But it isn't true. You loved this house far more than you ever loved me. You'll always love this house. So I packed my bags. I didn't want to go. Part of me prayed you'd try to stop me. That you'd say things could change. You didn't. So I left.'

'And I had no idea where you were, so even if I'd wanted to, I couldn't have come after you.

I didn't hear a word from you for five years, Pippa. I didn't know if you were alive or dead, happy or sad. I almost went out of my mind in the beginning. My heart was broken into pieces. I wasn't sure how I managed to stay alive. It was actually Olivia who got me through it. And this house.'

'Yours wasn't the only heart that was breaking. I almost went out of my mind too. In fact, I went a bit wild. I couldn't get in touch, Rafe. Don't you understand? I loved you. If I'd heard your voice, or seen your face, I would've come back in an instant. And I knew I couldn't do that. Because if I had, I wouldn't have survived. I'm not being melodramatic, Rafe. Your own father drank and drugged himself to death.'

'Please don't remind me of that.'

'I'm sorry. But I know exactly how he felt. If I'd come back, I honestly think it would've killed me. Mind you, being apart from you almost did the same, but I made some good friends and they helped me through the pain and heartache. I returned to Oxford. We'd been so happy there and I wanted to feel that happiness again. Probably not the wisest thing to do, but it actually did work out well. I started working in a club and I learnt more about the business of hospitality. I dated the owner and after a few years, I thought I might be over you. I sent the divorce papers, more to prove it to myself than anything. But I didn't want to remarry. At least not to anyone but you. I worked hard and eventually I managed to buy the nightclub from my then ex-boyfriend when he decided to retire early, to Jamaica. The rest, as they say, is history. But the truth is, Rafe. I never got over you. So here I am. Foolishly wondering, hoping, praying, that perhaps, it's not too late. That perhaps, you never quite got over me either.'

He couldn't comprehend what she was telling him. And yet he knew all of it was true.

'Why now, Pippa? Why after all these years have you decided now is the time to come back?'

She shrugged and slowly walked around his desk stopping just inches from him and gazing up at him with those big beautiful eyes. Eyes that once, he'd thought he'd drown in.

'I've thought about it lots of times over the years. This isn't a sudden decision. Or maybe it is. At least getting in the car and driving here this morning was. I hadn't planned that. I was actually going to go and stay with some friends for the weekend. I told you I'd heard about your gin. The truth is, I only heard about it last night. I was closing up the club, as I still do on occasion, and one of my team asked if I'd heard about this new gin. It was called Wyntersleap Gin and was made in an old barn on some estate, using the water from a local river, and I knew at once it was yours. I went home and read up all about it and decided I'd get in touch. The next thing I knew, I was in the car heading to Wynter House and phoning my friends to cancel. Luckily they're good friends and understood. That's it. That's why I'm here.'

He still didn't understand. Not entirely.

'To do a deal to stock our gin?'

'Oh, Rafe.' She took the tips of his shirt collar in her fingers and looked deep into his eyes. 'Yes. In part. But didn't you hear the bit about hoping you weren't over me? I want you back, Rafe. I want us to be together. I want us to be a team like we could've been all those years ago. I have money now. I'm actually quite well off. And people like Olivia don't frighten me one bit. If anything, I frighten them.' She gave a small laugh. 'I love you, Rafe Wynter. In fact, I think I've loved you all my life.'

Her heavenly scent pervaded his nostrils; her soft, sensual laugh was joyful to his ears. She still loved him. She always had. He'd misunderstood it all completely all those years ago. He'd been blind to what was happening around him. He'd been a complete and utter fool. He never thought Pippa would ever be in his arms again, yet here she was, asking him to take her back. Asking him to love her.

He'd imagined this moment for so, so many years.

Her lips parted as she inched closer. She

was about to kiss him. He remembered what it had felt like to be kissed by her and as her body leant against his, he reached up to touch her shapely hips.

'I still can't believe you're here,' he said, his voice little more than a whisper. 'This all feels so surreal.'

'I'm here, Rafe. And I'll be here for as long as you want me.'

Chapter Twenty-Three

'Oh God, Jo! I don't know what to do. I thought he'd come after me, but he hasn't.'

Neva's sobs were audible down the phone; she was clearly fighting back tears. She had told Jo she had called her the moment she was sure she was out of earshot of Rafe's study and Jo had managed to grasp the main points from Neva's garbled account of what had just happened.

'Why the hell did you leave them together?'

Jo mouthed an apology across the table to Ed, who smiled and mouthed back that it was OK, before winking and indicating with his hand that he'd be at the counter until she'd finished her conversation.

'I had to leave. I couldn't stay. I felt like a gooseberry and yet I'm his girlfriend. No. His fiancée!'

Neva had said that Pippa had poured her heart out to her in Rafe's study and that Neva had been genuinely moved by her story. Then

Rafe had appeared and said he'd heard it all and looked all doe-eyed at his ex and they'd acted as if they were about to forgive and forget the past and actually make things up between them. Even that sounded pretty worrying to Jo and she knew that probably wasn't the half of it.

'Then go back right now before they do make things up. I can't believe he didn't come after you though. That is a bit worrying. And you think she really was sincere?'

'Totally. And the worst part is, I sympathise with her. I can imagine how awful Olivia was and how hard it must've been for a nineteen-year-old to be faced with life at Wynter House.'

'I thought it was rather warm and welcoming, but I agree about Olivia.'

'It is warm and welcoming. Now. But I bet it wasn't when Olivia was in charge. But I don't care about the house. I think I'm losing Rafe and I don't know what to do. Everyone's been saying how important history is. You and Rob, Judith and Gavin, Cat and Amias. Rafe and I have less than two months' history. Two months, Jo! He and Pippa have an entire lifetime.'

'But not together. Didn't he tell you that they had a whirlwind romance and were only married for three years when she had an affair and left him?'

'Yes but they still loved one another for years after that. I told you he said it took him years to get over her. And maybe he's not over her. He thought she never loved him. Now he discovers she did. And she says she's not over him. Oh God. I haven't told you who she had the affair with. You're not going to believe this.'

'Adam?'

Neva gasped. 'How the hell did you guess that?'

'Because Adam's a flirt, and although he and Rafe clearly love one another dearly, there's still an atmosphere or something between them. Rafe started the distillery with a friend from the village. Not Adam. Although I know he's included him in it now. But isn't that only really recently? And Adam sometimes looks at Rafe as if he's half expecting to be told to get lost. I don't know. It's just a feeling I got when I was staying there. And it seems, as usual, I'm right. What's interesting is that Rafe's obviously forgiven Adam for the affair a long time ago, although maybe not completely, and yet he hasn't forgiven Pippa. I hate to say this, but holding on to that sort of hatred and resentment can sometimes be a way of hiding deeper feelings.'

'So you're telling me my fiancé still loves his ex-wife? Jesus Christ, Jo! What do I do?'

'You either go back in there and you ask him. Or you leave them to it and hope and pray that he comes to his senses and chooses you.'

'Comes to his senses? She was his wife. What if coming to his senses means going back with her?'

'Then the man's an idiot. And I don't think Rafe's an idiot. Whatever the gorgeous Pippa says and whatever excuses she comes up with, doesn't change the fact she cheated on him. And with his brother. And then she ran off and left him. Now you can say it's all some big heart-breaking, tear-jerking, life-long romance and that the pair of them are meant to be together. Or you can see it for what it really is. A woman in her late thirties, realising that she threw away the best thing she ever had, and trying to get it back. A woman who, when the going was really tough, got going. Only in the wrong direction. Instead of telling her husband to grow a pair, then supporting him and what he was trying to achieve, and telling the old bat Olivia to bugger off, she had a hissy fit, banged the brother, then ran off in search of better things. If Rafe takes her back, he deserves whatever he gets.'

'That's a bit harsh, Jo. As much as I don't want him to give her a second chance, I can see why she did what she did.'

'Bollocks! Answer me one thing. And be honest, Neva. I can remember you at nineteen. If you had been married to Rafe and found yourself at Wynter House with the dragon,

Olivia breathing fire down on you, would you have done what Pippa did? Any of it. The truth, please.'

Silence followed for a second or two during which Jo smiled at Ed who was giving her a concerned look.

'In your own time, Neva. But please don't take too long. My fish and chips are getting cold.'

'What? You're eating lunch? Sorry. Er. No. I would've stayed out of Olivia's way, made friends with all the staff so that they did some of the things I wanted, only without Olivia knowing, and told Rafe every day how much I loved him. I'd have found a job, or something I could do to help out at the house, and I'd have found ways for me and Rafe to spend more time together. But that's me and it might not have worked. I think he was a different person in some ways back then.'

'I'm sure he was. And that's another thing in your favour. He's changed. And he's told you more than once that's he's even changed since meeting you. He's more laid back. He's happier. He's in love. I honestly do believe he is, Neva. And it's with you, not his ex-wife. But I'm going to say this as your best friend. If Pippa's as gorgeous as you say she is, and if she's determined to get him back, there's a chance, a very slim one but nevertheless, a chance, he may be tempted to ... you know ...

see what he's been missing.'

'Have sex with her, you mean?'

'Yes. Just sex, Neva. It doesn't mean he loves her.'

'It does to me. I'd better get back to his study before that happens, because as much as I love him, I'm not sure I could forgive that.'

'Neva? Don't do anything stu–'

Ed raised his brows. 'She's hung up?'

Jo nodded. 'Yes.'

'Remind me not to get on the wrong side of you. You're one feisty lady.'

'I'm also a worried one. I really like you, Ed–'

'But you're concerned about your friend? It's OK. Go. Do what you've got to do. I'll be here when you get back.'

Jo leapt to her feet, leaving her fish and chips half-eaten, grabbed her coat and dashed towards the door but she stopped and ran back behind the counter, threw her arms around Ed's neck and kissed him full on the lips.

He quickly wrapped his arms around her, saying, 'Wow!' when she pulled away.

She grinned up at him as she eased herself out of his arms. 'Well, it was our second date. And I make it a rule to kiss a man I'm on a second date with. Are we still on for our third?'

'You betcha! Sorry. I'm still mesmerised by that kiss. I don't suppose I could have another, could I? I won't be so surprised next time.'

'You betcha!' she said, leaning in for a repeat of the first, which was possibly the best kiss she had ever had.

So far.

Chapter Twenty-Four

Neva took a deep breath, wiped her eyes and headed back towards Rafe's study. She had only been gone a few minutes. She could say she needed the loo. That sounded pathetic, but she didn't care. They probably wouldn't even ask. Or she could simply say she'd forgotten that she actually needed a word with Rafe. Which was true. She'd gone to his study to give him back his ring. Although, given what had just happened, that might not be the wisest thing to do at this precise time.

She was about to push the door open, which was still ajar from when she had left, but Rafe's voice stopped her in her tracks, her hand hovering in mid-air. His voice was soft but she could still make out each and every word, and each one made her feel as if she'd fallen head first into a food processor.

'I still can't believe you're here,' he said, his voice little more than a whisper. 'This all feels so surreal.'

'I'm here, Rafe,' Pippa replied in the sexist, sultriest tone on the planet. 'And I'll be here for as long as you want me.'

Neva clamped a hand over her mouth to stifle the scream she could feel bubbling up inside her. For a second she considered shoving the door open and catching them in the act of doing whatever it was they were about to do. Instead, she peered around the edge of the door and almost had a heart attack.

Pippa was standing right in front of Rafe and her arms were raised. Neva couldn't see Pippa's face or where her hands were because Rafe's broad shoulders and back blocked them out, but she could see Rafe's head was slightly bent, as if he were about to kiss Pippa. His arm slowly rose up as if he were about to take Pippa in it.

Neva had seen enough. She spun on her toes and fled. It was only when she had raced to the top of the stairs and was gasping for breath in the hall, that she let out a scream. Not a really loud one, but loud enough to be heard in the hall below and probably in one or two of the bedrooms. Not that she cared who heard it.

Rafe was now kissing Pippa, she was certain of that. And Neva's relationship with him was officially over.

She stormed along the hall to his room, ripped off his ring and although she'd initially been tempted to throw it, not caring where it landed, she stopped herself. It was important to him. She couldn't lose it. Instead, she placed it on his bedside table. Then she grabbed her overnight bag, which was in his wardrobe, threw all her clothes in it and marched back along the hall, once again fighting back her tears.

'Was that you, screaming like a banshee?'

Neva turned on her heel, clothes spilling from the top of her bag and glowered at Olivia.

'Yes, Olivia, it was. Because that's what we hairdressers do when our hearts have been broken in two.'

Olivia raised her brows and leant on her stick as Neva turned away.

'Are you going somewhere?'

Neva tutted loudly and stopped, spinning around again to glare at the woman a little more.

'Yes, Olivia. I am. I'm going home. And you'll be pleased to know, you won't be seeing me again.'

'Oh! Why not?'

Neva gave a tiny scream of frustration. Every time she went to leave, this bloody woman stopped her.

'Because, as you'll be pleased to hear, it's over between me and Rafe. I expect you'll finally go downstairs now, won't you? And no doubt have a big celebration. But I wouldn't get too excited if I were you. I may be going, but

Pippa is back, although I'm sure you knew that already. The thing you may not know is that Pippa will be staying. Probably for ever. Goodbye. Good luck. Thanks for making me feel oh so welcome in your beautiful home.'

'Wait! Did you hear me, Neva? Stop!'

Neva stopped. Mainly because she was so surprised Olivia had actually used her name. She turned round slowly and met Olivia's stare.

'Why is it over between you and my grandson? And what makes you think that woman will be staying, permanently or otherwise?'

Neva sucked in a breath. 'That woman has a name, Olivia. I may not like her, but she deserves some respect. And she's staying because Rafe is taking her back.'

Olivia looked genuinely astonished.

'That I do not believe, for one minute. As for respect. She had an affair, whilst married to Rafe, with Adam, no less, and you believe she deserves respect? Even though you think she's trying to steal the man you say you love?'

'Yes. Because if it hadn't been for you, she would never have left in the first place.'

'Me? I had nothing to do with her leaving.'

Neva blinked several times. 'You're amazing, Olivia. And not in a good way.'

'So you're leaving? Just like that? You're not going to stay and try to fight for him? I thought you said you loved Rafe.'

'I love him more than you could ever imagine. That's why I'm leaving. I want him to be happy. If that means him being with someone else, then as much as it breaks my heart, I have to accept that. If you love someone. Truly love them. You shouldn't have to fight for them. And they shouldn't want you to. Love is about respect and trust and wanting to spend your life with someone. Wanting to make them as happy as they make you. There's no point in trying to make someone love you if they don't. Or if they love someone else.'

'You're saying you don't trust Rafe? You're telling me he doesn't love you?' Olivia snorted derisively.

'I'm saying that when you see the man you love about to kiss his ex-wife, it's time for you to leave. I don't want to make him have to choose between us. What good would that do? Especially as he'd clearly choose her.'

'Kiss Pippa? You saw Rafe kiss Pippa? You're lying and I don't know why.'

'I am not lying, Olivia. They're in his study, and by now they could be doing a whole lot more than kissing. But I'm not going to go down that route. I'm off. Before I lose my mind completely, and do something stupid I'll regret. Goodbye.'

'You're a coward. Which surprises me almost as much as you saying Rafe is kissing Pippa.'

Neva sighed. 'OK. Fine. I know you've recently had a heart attack, Olivia and I know your world has been turned upside down what with the villagers, me and my family, me dating Rafe, Adam dating Hazel, and now Cat and Kyra becoming part of this family, but I have to say this, so buckle up. It's going to be a bumpy ride. In fact, let me get you a chair.'

Neva dropped her bag and grabbed one of a number of chairs which lined the hall, spaced several feet apart. She took it to Olivia and held it firm while looking her directly in the eye.

'Sit.'

Olivia sat, and stared at Neva, open mouthed.

Neva took a deep breath. 'You've been nothing but rude and ill-mannered to me and my family, not to mention the villagers. Most of whom still love you. God alone knows why. You're the most unlovable person I've ever met. But they do. Apart from Ethel. You run poor Judith ragged. You treated Hazel like dirt, and you still do despite the fact she nursed you back to health and undoubtedly saved Adam's life. You think you can snap your fingers and everyone will do your bidding. You've got a wonderful, beautiful, lovely and kind granddaughter and great-granddaughter whom you're too stubborn and pig-headed to meet. Your grandsons adore you, and you treat them like little children, when you can be bothered to pay them any attention at all, that is. You're more concerned with what others may think of the family name when in all honesty, no one even gives a damn about the Wynter name. Sorry, but it's true. And now I find out that you treated Pippa the same, and made her life a misery. You undermined her and made her look foolish. You probably even lied about her to Rafe.'

'I did not!'

'Fine. Ethel told me that when you came here as Sebastian's bride you were beautiful, inside and out. You turned ugly after his death and you want to make everything around you ugly too. Well you won't succeed. Love isn't ugly, Olivia. Love is beautiful and wonderful and it's a gift. A gift we may not have for long. Not in your case, and clearly not in mine. But it's still a gift. I wonder what Sebastian would say if he could see you now. I bet he wouldn't recognise the woman he fell in love with. Right. That's it. I've said my piece. Don't bother to have me thrown out. I'll make my own way. Try to be kind, Olivia, even if it kills you. And welcome Pippa back, no matter how you feel. Rafe deserves to be happy. And so does Adam. Oddly enough, so do you.'

Neva picked up her bag and marched down the hall, with Olivia calling out her name in ever increasing tones. Neva did give one quick look back over her shoulder, just to check the woman wasn't having another heart attack. She wasn't. She was standing up and banging her stick on the floor. Neva could still hear it as she closed the front door of Wynter House behind her.

Hazel was in the drive, throwing her own bags into the back of her car and looking rather sad.

'Hazel? Are you leaving too? Have you and Adam broken up?'

Hazel gave her an odd look. 'Not exactly. But we have had a fight. Hold on. Are you leaving?'

Neva nodded. Now that she had vented her anger at Olivia, she was beginning to feel tearful again and she didn't want that. She needed to be strong.

'Yes. It's a long story. Damn. I've just remembered, I haven't got my car here. Is there any chance you could give me a lift into Merriment Bay?'

'Sure thing.' Hazel re-opened the boot. 'Chuck your bag in the back. Wait. Is that Olivia screaming? Should I–?'

'No. She's fine. Trust me on that. But I'd like to get out of here before all hell breaks loose.'

Hazel looked a little unsure. 'I suppose Adam will text me if they need me.'

'Yep. Can we go please?'

Neva got into the passenger seat and Hazel

186

got in, started the car and headed down the drive.

'You haven't stolen the family silver, have you?' Hazel grinned wanly at Neva.

'Damn. I knew there was something I forgot.' She forced a smile. 'No. I just told Olivia a few things she didn't want to hear. Why have you and Adam had a fight? If you'd rather I mind my own business, I'll understand.'

'No. It's fine. I've got a new assignment and Adam's not too happy about it. Especially as it's a live-in post and it's likely to be long-term.'

'Oh I see. Is it far away?'

'Not that far. About twenty miles or so.'

'That's not too bad. You can still see one another during your time off. I suppose he's upset because it means you won't be spending every night together. But he knew you'd be getting another assignment soon, didn't he? You took some leave, didn't you, so he must've known you'd be going back to work fairly soon.'

'I think he was hoping I might not. But it's not so much the fact that I'm going back to work, as the person who I'm going to be looking after.'

'Oh? Why? Does he know them?'

'He knows of him. Because I foolishly told him. Do you remember last week when I told you about my ex-boyfriend, the policeman?'

'Yes. Oh God no! Please don't tell me it's him!'

'It is. I specialise in geriatric nursing but throughout my career I've cared for patients of all ages and with a variety of illnesses, long-term and life-limiting conditions, and disabilities. Jason's had a dreadful accident on his motorbike and is in a rather bad way. He's going to have to have several operations on his legs over a period of time and each one means he'll need to be properly looked after in between. He's been in hospital since the day I sent him that text. Can you believe that? The accident wasn't because of my text, by the way. Someone drove into him. But all the time I was nursing Olivia and then Adam back to health, Jason was lying in hospital in London. They're going to let him go home tomorrow and see how he goes. And out of the blue, he's suddenly asked for me. Someone else was due to take care of him but I got a call today. I did think about saying no but the thing is ... well, in a way ...'

'You still love him.' Neva let her head drop back against the headrest. 'What it is about former loves?'

'I don't know. Maybe it's the history. It doesn't mean I don't love Adam because I do. And I want our relationship to continue. But I'm not sure Adam trusts me. We've left things a bit up in the air. He asked me not to go and I said I had to. Oh God, Neva! You're crying.'

Neva wiped her eyes with the sleeve of her

188

jumper and sobbed, 'Rafe's going to take Pippa back and I think my heart is breaking.'

Chapter Twenty-Five

'No.' Rafe's lips brushed against Pippa's and he immediately backed away, shaking his head to try to snap himself out of what had felt like some sort of trance. He raked a hand through his hair, letting his other hand which had skimmed her hip, fall to his side. 'I'm sorry, Pippa. I can't do this. I don't know what came over me.'

He stepped away, a little worried that he might get sucked back into the strange dream-like state he had obviously been in. What other explanation was there? He had almost kissed his ex-wife.

Almost.

Thank God he hadn't. How could he even think of doing that to Neva?

And why on earth hadn't he gone after Neva when she left?

Because he'd been so astonished by Pippa's revelations? Because he'd wanted to hear her explanation? But why? All that happened years ago. What difference did it really make?

OK. If all the things Pippa said were true, there might have been a possibility that they might not have broken up. But it was only a slight possibility, and in any event, it was water under the bridge.

Water under the bridge. That made him smile. He remembered the first time he'd seen Neva. She was running down the High Street of Wyntersleap in torrential rain, chasing a puppy the size of a wolf with her young niece running behind her.

It might not have been love at first sight, exactly, but he had known the minute he walked towards her, having saved the puppy, that she was going to be important in his life. She'd certainly stirred up some very strong emotions in him. And not just that day. Each time he saw her after that, he'd felt things he hadn't felt in a very long time. Ever, in fact. It hadn't taken him long to fall in love. Deeply in love.

'Rafe?' Pippa's voice broke in on his thoughts. 'What's wrong?'

He beamed at her. 'Nothing's wrong, Pippa. But everything almost was. I'm in love. Deeply, passionately and no doubt completely for the rest of my life. But I'm afraid it's not with you. It's with Neva.'

'Neva?' She shook her head and leant back

against the edge of his desk as if she suddenly found it hard to stand. 'I shouldn't have come.'

'No. You probably shouldn't have. But in an odd way, I'm glad you did. I think a part of me still harboured a bit of animosity towards you and maybe even a tiny bit of the love I'd once felt for you. Hearing everything you said has made me realise the breakdown of our marriage was as much my fault, as yours. That was something I needed to hear. And it's a mistake I'm not going to make a second time.'

'A second time?' She looked a little shaken.

'I'm sorry, Pippa. I'm not saying these things to hurt you. Truly I'm not. But I think you should know that Neva and I are going to be married.'

'Married?' She made a sound as if she were in pain. 'I'd like to say that it's a bit sudden but you married me almost as fast.'

'I never thought I'd marry again. I didn't even want to. Until I met Neva. I can't explain it, Pippa, but this time I know it will last. This time it's for life. Because I'm going to do anything and everything to damn well make sure it does.'

'There's nothing I can say or do to change your mind?'

He shook his head. 'No. There isn't. Wait. Did you just hear a scream?'

'No. Perhaps it's the foxes. I remember when I first heard them they terrified me.'

He strained his ears but there was only silence.

'Yes. I remember. Er. You can still stay, if you like. But you may decide you'd rather go and see your friends, after all.'

'I think I should go and see my friends, don't you?'

He smiled at her and nodded. 'I think that may be for the best. But there's no rush.'

'She's a very lucky girl, Rafe.'

'No, Pippa. I'm the lucky one. But even I hadn't realised quite how lucky until today.'

'Er. Can we still do business together? Can my nightclubs still stock your gin?'

'I'd like that. But I'd like to run it by Neva, first. I don't want her to feel uncomfortable. And even assuming she doesn't mind, I feel it might be best if you dealt with Sean, or even Adam instead of me.'

'Fair enough. I really am sorry for the way it all worked out back then, Rafe. For the things I said and did, and for the things I didn't say or do. But it wasn't all bad, was it?'

'No. It wasn't all bad. It was good. Very good. Just not as good as now. You're going to be OK, aren't you?'

She nodded. 'Yes. I think a large part of me knew what the answer was going to be, but I had to try.'

'You'll find someone who loves you the way I love Neva, Pippa. I know you will.'

'I hope so, Rafe.'

'I need to go. I want to go and find her. It must have been rather strange standing there and listening to us discussing our past. I'm not surprised she left us to it. I want to make sure she's OK. Is that all right? If I leave you here, I mean.'

She pushed herself away from his desk.

'Not here. There are too many memories in this room for me. I'll walk out with you. I think, perhaps, I owe your girlfriend an apology.'

'Actually, she's not my girlfriend. She's my fiancée. We got engaged last night but I don't think either of us wanted to spoil Judith and Gavin's day. We'll announce our engagement tomorrow.'

'Engaged? I know you said you were getting married but I didn't realise you'd already asked her. Why didn't she just tell me that?'

'Perhaps she thought it should come from me.'

'Possibly. Oh. What's this about you having a sister and a niece?'

'Who told you about that?' He smiled. He didn't mind that she knew. He would've told her himself over the weekend.

'Neva.'

'Neva? How strange that she should tell you about Cat and Kyra but not that she and I are engaged.' He laughed. 'Sometimes I have no idea what is going on in her head, but I love her all the more for that. She keeps me on my toes. OK. That was definitely a scream. And it sounds like Olivia is screaming Neva's name.' Fear engulfed him. 'Oh God.'

He ran along the corridor from his study towards the hall and saw Archie hurrying towards him.

'Archie? What's happened? Is Neva OK? Why is Olivia screaming her name? And now mine? What's going on?'

'I believe Neva has had words with Olivia. And I may be wrong, but I understand that Neva and Hazel have left Wynter House. Oh. I apologise, Mr Rafe I wasn't aware—'

'Drop the formality, Archie. Pippa doesn't care about it anymore than I do. What do you mean, Neva had words with Olivia? And by "left the house" do you mean they've gone outside? Or are you suggesting something more serious?'

'I believe Neva told Olivia what she thought of her, Rafe, and yes, something far more serious.'

Chapter Twenty-Six

Rafe raced towards the stairs and saw that Olivia was slowly making her way down, yelling his name like an old fishwife. Not the way Olivia usually behaved. Adam appeared a few steps above her, looking exceedingly grumpy, and Cecil and Ronnie, Ethel and Queenie, and well, everyone was now congregating in the hall.

'What is going on, Olivia? Adam? What's all this about? And where is Neva? Archie says she's left the house. Is that true? Has anybody seen her?'

'She's left,' Olivia snapped. 'And it's all her fault.'

She pointed her stick at Pippa and swayed as if she might topple down the stairs. Fortunately, Adam dashed down and caught her, steadying her with both hands.

'Careful, Olivia,' Adam said. 'Hazel's gone, so we don't have a nurse if you tumble and break your neck.'

'Don't tell me she's also left? What is the matter with you two? And this is just as much your fault, Rafe. I expected better of you. Although I still do not believe it. I need a word with you.'

'I'm afraid I don't have the time, Olivia. I need to find Neva.'

'Make time!' Olivia banged her stick on the stair.

'I saw Neva leave with Hazel,' Penny said. 'About five minutes ago, I think. She had her overnight bag. They both did.'

'Her bag? With Hazel?' He looked up at Adam. 'Where's Hazel gone, Adam?'

'To live with her ex-boyfriend.'

'What?' Everyone in the hall spoke in unison.

'To nurse him back to health, I meant. He's had an accident. Although things don't look too good for our relationship right now. I have no idea why Neva went with her though. Or where they are. What does Olivia mean that it's your fault and Pippa's?'

'Neva says she saw Rafe kiss her,' Olivia said.

'What?' Now Rafe and Pippa spoke together and stared at one another.

'I didn't kiss Pippa.'

'I didn't believe you did, but Neva was adamant she saw you. Are you simply going to manhandle me Adam or are you actually intending to help me down these stairs?'

Adam looked at Olivia and at Rafe. He then bent down and lifted Olivia into his arms. She let out a tiny shriek but he carried her down the stairs and stood her on her feet at the bottom.

'Why did Neva tell you that?' Rafe asked as they were descending. 'I understood that the pair of you rarely speak to one another.'

'We didn't.' Olivia glared at Adam and smoothed down her dress. 'Well, help me to a chair then. And don't for one minute contemplate sweeping me off my feet again. Those days are over for me, my boy.'

Adam tutted and led her by the arm to one of the chairs in the hall while Rafe continued his questioning.

'Olivia, please will you tell me precisely what happened? What did Neva say, exactly?'

'Far too much for me to repeat. And not very much of it was pleasant.'

'She was upset. If she thought I'd kissed Pippa I think that's understandable.'

'I didn't say it wasn't.' She glanced around him. 'Are you still here, Pippa?'

'Olivia!' Rafe snapped.

'Don't worry. I'm just leaving,' Pippa said. 'I hope you sort this out, Rafe. You've got my number if you need me to persuade Neva you didn't kiss me. There's no point in us all being miserable.'

'Pippa!' Olivia banged her stick against the

floor. 'Neva tells me I treated you badly and that I was wrong to do so. I don't agree with that, but if I did, I apologise. You may stay if you wish, but I think it's best for everyone if you leave.'

'You just asked her to leave.' Rafe was utterly bewildered now. And he couldn't quite believe that Olivia had apologised.

'No. I asked if she was still here? I couldn't see her. You were standing in the way. Now, I have one or two things to say to you, Rafe. It's entirely up to you if you want everyone here to hear them.'

'All I want to hear is where Neva has gone.'

'You're a fool, Rafe.'

'Olivia, I don't intend to have this conversation, now or ever again. I know how you feel about Neva but I have news for you. Neva and I are engaged. At least I hope to God we still are. I'm going to marry her, if I have my way.'

Everyone gasped then started to clap and cheer but it soon faded out when Olivia spoke.

'She wasn't wearing a ring when she hauled me over the coals. I would've noticed.'

'She's wearing my signet ring.'

'She wasn't when she left. And why in God's name did you give her your signet ring?'

'Because that's all I had to hand last night. I love her, Olivia. How many more times do I need to tell you this?'

'It's not me you need to convince. It's Neva. She didn't tell me you were engaged. Here. Give her this. She may not want it, but it'll do until she chooses one she does want.' She eased the massive sapphire and diamond engagement ring Rafe's grandfather, Sebastian had given her, slowly from her finger and held it out to him. He stared at it, at Adam and then back at Olivia.

'You're giving Neva your engagement ring?'

Olivia snorted. 'Don't be a fool, Rafe. You're giving her my engagement ring. And tell her it's a family heirloom.' She laughed. 'Although I don't suppose that'll impress her much at all. But it's the least the future wife of the head of the Wynter family deserves. Now for goodness sake, go and find her. And don't ask again where she is. She's obviously gone to see her best friend, Jo. Or possibly to her parents' house. Either way, I believe you'll find her in Merriment Bay. If you leave now, perhaps she'll be back in time for dinner. We eat at 8 at Wynter House. Oh. Until the new Mrs Wynter says otherwise.'

Rafe took the ring from her and stared at it in disbelief. Was this actually happening?

Olivia patted his hand, looked away and continued: 'Now will someone please make me a cup of tea. I'm parched. And Judith? I believe I owe you and Gavin my congratulations. I assume you'll be married in the chapel. That goes for you, Rafe. I assume, this time, you'll hold your wedding at Wynter House. But why are you still here? I thought you were going after the woman you love.'

Rafe shook his head. 'Is this all some strange dream? Are you saying you're giving us your blessing? What's caused this sudden change of heart? Are you honestly saying I should give this ring to Neva?'

'That girl's got gumption, Rafe,' Olivia said, smiling at him. 'That's what the wife of a Wynter needs. Gumption. She told me a few things I needed to hear. But what is really important is that she's prepared to put your happiness before her own, even if it breaks her heart. That's true love. I like her. Go and bring her back to Wynter House.'

Chapter Twenty-Seven

Rafe raced out of Wynter House, although he still wasn't totally convinced this wasn't all a dream. He half expected to wake up and find Neva curled up against him, still wearing his signet ring, and with no trace of Pippa anywhere. Perhaps the fact that Neva had proposed had brought up something from his subconscious.

But when Jo almost ran him over on the drive, and shouted at him, he was pretty sure he was awake.

'Where are you going, you bastard?'

'To find Neva. Is she at the flat?'

'No. She's here.'

'She's not. She left about five minutes or so ago with Hazel. I'm just going to find her to bring her back.'

'Damn. I must have driven past them. Where's your ex?'

'She's leaving.'

'Did you kiss her?'

'No, Jo. I did not. But Neva thinks I did and I really need to explain what happened. Excuse me.'

'Get in. I'll drive.'

He hesitated for a nanosecond before jumping into her car and she sped down the drive as if her life depended on it.

'You'd better not be lying,' Jo said. 'Because I'll kill you if you are.'

'I'm not. I promise you. But I will admit, I almost did kiss Pippa. I have no idea why.'

'You'd better think of something better to say than that.'

'I'd rather be honest.'

'You're a fool.'

'Why does everyone keep saying that? And why? For being honest?'

'For even thinking about kissing your ex. Neva loves you so much and I'm not sure you deserve her. I thought you did. Now I don't know.'

'I adore her, Jo. I can't imagine my life without her.'

'That's better. Say that. I was in the middle of a date when all this blew up, you know. I haven't had sex for ages and I'd just started a date with the most fantastic guy, then you behave like a plonker.'

'I'm sorry. I'll try to make it up to you.'

'Just promise me you won't do it again.'

'I won't. Er. But I would like to get to Neva, alive.'

'Don't be a wimp. I'm not going that fast. Why is Neva in Hazel's car?'

'Because Hazel's left Wynter House to go and nurse her ex-boyfriend back to health.'

'Her ex-boyfriend? Really? What's wrong with him?'

'He's had an accident.'

'What sort of accident?'

'I have no idea. I was too busy trying to ascertain what Neva said to Olivia and where she was now, to enquire.'

'Neva said something to Olivia?'

'Several things, I understand. Look. I think that's Hazel's car.'

'Wow. It's all been happening at Wynter House today. I'm almost sorry I missed it.'

Jo pulled up sharply right behind Hazel's car and Neva spun round in surprise. She obviously spotted Rafe because she stumbled backwards as if in shock and he dashed from the car and reached out for her.

'Rafe! Please go away. I can't do this right now.'

'I have something I need to tell you,' he pleaded.

'Are you OK?' Hazel asked from her driver's seat, via the open window.

'He didn't kiss her,' Jo yelled from hers.

Neva nodded at Hazel before glancing around Rafe's body to look at Jo. 'He did. I saw him.'

'No. You only saw—'

'Thank you, Jo,' Rafe said. 'But I think it's best if I do the explaining.'

'Then I hope you make a better job of it than earlier. Neva. I'll be in The Perfect Plaice if you need me.' She leant further out of the car window. 'Hazel, are you off? I hear Jason's had an accident. Is he OK?'

Hazel leant out of her window, twisting round in her seat. 'He'll live. But he's in a bad way. I'm going to take care of him.'

'Give us a call soon then.' Jo waved at Hazel.

'You're leaving?' Neva asked Jo.

'I'll only be a few doors away. Give the man a chance. I actually believe him.'

'Shall I stay?' Hazel asked.

Neva glanced at Jo and at Rafe before shaking her head.

'No, thank you, Hazel. I think I'll be OK. But please give us a call very soon, as Jo said.'

Hazel waved, tooted her horn and drove forward down Coast Road. Jo gave a thumbs up and reversed backwards. Rafe stood on the pavement looking at Neva, still not quite sure precisely what was going on.

She met his eyes briefly before lowering her gaze.

'If you're here to say you're sorry but you can't help your feelings, please don't. I understand. But I'd rather not hear excuses or apologies. I know how much you loved her, and clearly still do. I don't think I can bear to hear you say it though. These things happen. I'll get over it. Eventually.'

Her voice shook as she spoke and he reached out and took her hands in his. She tried to pull away but he held them firmly but gently.

'I am sorry. And I can't help my feelings. But they're not for Pippa, Neva. They're for you. You're the woman I love. I know you think you saw us kiss, but we didn't. I swear to you. I'm not here to make excuses but I truly want to apologise because you're right. No. I didn't kiss Pippa before you say again that I did. But for a second. No. Less than a second. For the briefest amount of time, I thought I was going to. I have no idea why. Jo told me not to say that, but it's true. I don't want to lie to you, Neva. I think it was because a part of me didn't believe it was real. I didn't believe she was there. I haven't seen her for years and then suddenly, there she is. And she looked better than I remembered. That sounds awful, I know. But that's what I thought. That didn't mean I fell back in love with her. It didn't mean I wanted her. It simply means she looked better than I remembered.'

'She's beautiful. I can't blame you for thinking that. Do you mean it, Rafe? Is it really me you love, not Pippa?'

'She's nothing compared to you, Neva. I mean that. And yes. I love you. Completely and utterly. I told you once that I'd never been jealous of Adam before. But that when I thought it was him you wanted, I was eaten up with jealousy. And it wasn't a pleasant feeling. Or something I'd experienced. Not even when Pippa had her affair. I told you I didn't feel jealous of her lover. Well now you know who her lover was, so that should tell you something. I told you all I felt then was disappointment in her and heartbreak because our marriage was over. Do you remember that?'

She nodded. 'Yes I do.'

'And I think I also told you then that I didn't want there to be any secrets between us. Ever.'

'Yes. I remember that.'

'So I'm telling you the complete and honest truth because I meant that then and I mean it now. Seeing Pippa again was actually a good thing. I told her this and I'm telling you. I think I might have still been holding on to a few residual feelings. Lost dreams, maybe. I don't know. I've often wondered how I would feel if I ever saw her again. I was so happy this morning when I woke up and I think some of the happiness I felt seeped over when I saw her. I didn't feel angry, or hurt, or anything. All I felt was happy. And that was because of you. Then I heard her say all those things and those residual feelings sort of came to the surface. It was almost as if you weren't there and it was Pippa and me, way back then, when we were still together. She asked me today if we could get back together and she leant in to kiss me and I almost kissed her. But it wasn't the Pippa today I was about to kiss. It was the one from all those years ago. Does that make any sense to you at all?'

'In a way. I think everyone is drawn back to history. But did you kiss her, Rafe? Be honest.'

'No. My lips brushed hers. Just brushed. And my hand skimmed her hip but I immediately pulled away and stepped back from her when I realised what was happening. It was as if I'd been in some sort of trance. I told her it wasn't going to happen and that I'd almost made a terrible mistake. I told her I loved you. Love you. And that you're the only woman for me.'

'Is this true, Rafe? Is it really true?'

He nodded and held her gaze. 'It's true.'

She beamed at him but her smile quickly vanished.

'What happened after that? You were still in your study when I left. I'm pretty sure of that.'

'Nothing happened. We talked. I told her I'll only do business with her if you agree, and that even then, she can deal with Sean or Adam. I have no intention of seeing her again. Not because I'm afraid to, before you suggest that. I'm now one hundred and ten per cent positive that all I feel for her is friendship. And not even that, really. Pippa is my past. She won't be a part of my future. I told her we're engaged and I plan to marry you. If you'll still have me. And if you won't. I'm not going anywhere. I'll win you back no matter how long it takes. Will you forgive me, Neva? For being a fool for a moment and for almost making the biggest mistake of my life.'

Neva gasped and the smile came back. 'You're not a fool, Rafe. But I did take off your ring. It's on your bedside table. And before we go any further, there's something I need to tell you. I said some rather unpleasant things to Olivia. I don't think she'll ever want me back at Wynter House.'

He smiled and got down on one knee, taking Olivia's ring from the pocket of his jeans.

Neva looked around and a passing car tooted its horn, but Rafe didn't care.

'That's where you're wrong. Olivia thinks you have gumption. She gave me her engagement ring so that you would at least have something special to wear. If you don't like it, you can choose your own. I know you proposed to me last night, but you said you didn't really mean it. I'm proposing to you now, and I do mean it, Neva. I love you with all my heart. I love you more than I love Wynter House. And I never thought I would love anyone more than that. I know this isn't the most romantic way to propose, but I need to know right now. Will you make me happy again, Neva? Will you be my wife?'

He held out Olivia's ring and it sparkled in the afternoon sunlight.

'That's Olivia's engagement ring? And she told you to give it to me?' She was clearly incredulous.

'Yes. Will you accept it?'

'Oh yes, Rafe, yes. Yes. I will. I want to marry you more than anything.'

She stretched out her left hand and he slid the ring on her finger. Like his signet ring, it was the perfect fit and he beamed at her before getting to his feet, sweeping her into his arms and kissing her, slowly spinning round and round.

More horns tooted. A couple passing by clapped and cheered. But all he could think about was Neva, and how lucky he was to have found the love of his life.

Chapter Twenty-Eight

Rome wasn't built in a day, and Neva didn't expect Olivia to change overnight, but the change in her was nothing short of a miracle. She was waiting in the drawing room of Wynter House when Neva and Rafe finally returned, after a quick detour to Neva's flat to have make-up and celebratory engagement sex. Rafe, understandably, didn't want to do that on the street.

They also popped in briefly to The Perfect Plaice so that Neva could tell Jo the engagement was back on, and so that she could meet Ed. Rafe and Ed got on so well, Rafe invited him and Jo up to Wynter House for drinks and dinner that night, and they said yes, although Jo did tell Neva when Ed was showing Rafe how the fryers worked, that the flat was out of bounds all day on Sunday.

'So if you and Rafe fall out again, you'll have to go and stay with your parents. Ed and I are having sex, and we may be there all day.

Which reminds me. I must text Rob and tell him not to come down.'

Neva tutted. 'We are never falling out again. Ever.'

'We could have fish and chips at our engagement party,' Rafe said.

'That's a great idea.' She nudged Jo. 'You see we agree on everything.'

'We need to organise that and to plan our wedding.' Rafe looked lovingly at Neva. 'What do you think about having the wedding in our chapel? I know that would make Olivia very happy, but it's up to you. And if you wanted to wear her wedding dress, that would be even better.'

Neva glanced at Jo. 'OK. We may fall out again.' She smiled at Rafe. 'I love the idea of the chapel. The dress, not so much. We just need to set a date. And we must remember, Judith and Gavin got engaged before us, so they should get first choice.'

'I was joking about the dress.' Rafe laughed as he and Ed rejoined Neva and Jo at the table. 'But we could all get married at the same time.'

'Please stop talking,' Jo said.

The first thing Neva did when they returned to Wynter House that afternoon was to go into the drawing room to see Olivia. She was nervous, of course, but Rafe held her hand.

'Just in time for tea,' Olivia said, beaming at them.

Was Neva imagining this? She looked at Rafe and his eyes were filled with love and admiration.

'I have something to say, Olivia.' Neva smiled even though her insides were shaking just a little.

'There's more?' Olivia looked her in the eye. 'Then come and sit beside me and say it.'

Neva walked over to Olivia's armchair by the fire and to everyone's surprise, including Neva's, she bent down and kissed Olivia on the cheek. Olivia blushed and her eyes gleamed with emotion. She coughed lightly and shot a look at Rafe.

'This girl is dangerous, Rafe. She'll have me inviting the Devons for dinner before I know it.'

Neva smiled again. 'I think that's a wonderful idea. I can hand deliver the invitation any time you like. I want to thank you for allowing me to wear your beautiful ring, Olivia. It's a perfect fit.' She held out her left hand so that Olivia could see it. 'I promise to take good care of it. It means the world to me.'

'If you really like it, you can keep it. It suits your hand. But you should also have another, of your own. With the gin business taking off, I'm sure Rafe can afford something beautiful before too long.'

Neva shook her head. 'I don't want another ring. If you're really happy for me to keep this one, I'd be thrilled. It makes our engagement even more special.'

Olivia patted Neva's hand. 'Then keep it, Neva. With mine and Sebastian's blessings. He would have liked you.'

'Thank you. That means a lot. I apologise for earlier. Not for the things I said but for the way I said them.'

Olivia met her eye. 'They needed to be said. And by someone other than my grandsons. The heart attack, and Adam's illness were a slight wake-up call, not to mention Rafe's threat to send me to live elsewhere, but for some strange reason, the things you said today, together with the way you said them, hit home. Sebastian would hate to see what I've allowed myself to become. Eaten up with bitterness and sorrow. I need to let the sunshine in again. To see the good in people, just as he did, and as Rafe and Adam do. I saw the good in you today, young lady. And I saw that you love Rafe as much as I loved Sebastian. Don't think this means I won't try to boss you around because I shall. I have no doubt about that. But if you feel I've overstepped the mark, I know I can count on you to say so.'

'I'm so happy to hear you say that. You can definitely count on me.'

'And perhaps, if you're not too busy, you could do something with my hair. It looks such a fright and as I have two weddings to attend in the near future, I need to look my best.'

'I'll be happy to. Anytime.'

Neva looked at Rafe and the smile on his face said far more than words. The two women he loved most in the world were finally getting on. And there was a very good chance they may actually like one another.

Chapter Twenty-Nine

'You're saying we've got three big events to arrange,' Jo said, in the salon on Monday morning, 'and only a matter of weeks in which to arrange them?' She had spent all of Sunday and Sunday night with Ed and she was struggling to keep her eyes open.

Neva beamed at her. 'Yep. And we need to fit it all in without clashing with the launch of Wyntersleap Gin. Won't this be fun?'

'Fun isn't the first word that springs to mind. Which one are we doing first, and has Rafe picked a date for the gin launch?'

'Yes. For the 29th of February. I think our salon opening should come first. Merriment Bay has spent far too long without a hairdressing and beauty salon. Let's organise that for this weekend. Everything's done now. It's just a matter of putting the stock on display and opening the door.'

'Friday or Saturday?'

'Saturday the 22nd. Let's have an open day.

Literally. We'll have cakes and champagne and we can invite people in for a mini treatment, and a wash and blow dry. Trims, but not restyling or tinting because they'd take too long. And we can give discount vouchers to those who book an appointment.'

'Great. That's that one sorted.'

'We'll need to do more planning than that.'

'Yeah, yeah. Next?'

'The engagement party, obviously. We're thinking of having a joint one of those, for us and Judith and Gavin. So that will be at Wynter House. Penny, Wendy and Taryn, with help from my mum and of course, my darling sister who is coming down to stay for that weekend, whenever it is, will do the food. Taryn will sing and we'll have lots of drinks, including the gin, and dancing.'

'Great. That's that organised. What if we have our open day and your engagement party on the same day? We could open from 9 till 3, or something, which leaves plenty of time to rest, before making yourself beautiful. Then we can all go up to Wynter House. That way your sister can help with both, and it'll save time.'

'But we need to send out invitations!'

'Who to? Everyone you want to come lives in Wynter House or in Merriment Bay. Unless Rafe and Olivia want to invite all and sundry. All we need to do is tell the vicar and, as Rafe told us before, the entire village will know within a matter of days. If you insist on having posh invitations, they can be delivered by hand.'

'No. We all just want a small engagement party. Mainly for our families and close friends of Rafe's, like Will Lester and Rory. Amias will come with Cat, of course. So I suppose you're right. It won't take that much organising.'

'Great. So that just leaves your wedding. Have Judith and Gavin set their date?'

'Yes. For Saturday the 7th of March.'

'Bloody hell. That's less than three weeks away. Not long to organise that then.'

'No. But neither of them has any family. Which is terribly sad, don't you think? And now that they're together, they want to marry right away. They were thinking of making it sooner.'

'OK. So when are you and Rafe thinking of having yours?'

'Er. The week after theirs. The 14th of March. I know that seems a bit rushed, but I don't want a big wedding and I know it sounds silly but I want to be Mrs Wynter as soon as possible.'

'Worried the other one might come back for one last try?'

'No. I just want to be Rafe's wife. More than anything in the world. And the sooner the better. We both agree on that. Judith and Gavin are going up to the Lake District for a few days for their honeymoon so they'll be back in time for ours. And Rafe is going to be re-opening Wynter House to the public at the end of March, so we want ours to be before that. Besides, it's at the chapel at Wynter House, as is Judith and Gavin's, so we can pick any date we want. Rafe checked this morning that Reverend Raine is free for both, and he is, so that's settled. We're going to have marquees in the grounds, but if the weather's bad, we can move everything back inside the house. I think it'll be perfect. And as Olivia said to us last night, she isn't getting any younger. I want her to be at our wedding and to enjoy it. I can't see any point in waiting.'

'I can't believe the difference in her. It's as if she's had a complete transformation.'

'I know. Although, not complete. She did tell me last night that I might want to consider improving my wardrobe when I become Mrs Wynter.'

Jo laughed. 'I couldn't believe how friendly she was to me and to Ed on Saturday night. Although I swear I saw her lip curl when Ed told her he owned The Perfect Plaice, as if having the owner of a fish and chip shop sitting at the dining table at Wynter House with Olivia Wynter, was just a bit of a stretch too far.'

'I know.' Neva laughed too. 'At least she went back to her rooms after dinner. I think, after being horrid for so long, it's going to wear her out being nice to people. She went to bed early last night as well. I hope she's OK. I hadn't thought about it but maybe this is all too much for her to handle.'

'Stop that right now. Don't start seeing problems that aren't there. OK then. We've got the dates for everything. Let's get cracking on sending out the wedding invitations.'

Chapter Thirty

By Saturday morning, Neva was beginning to feel worn out. She and her mum, together with Jo had spent the entire week dashing about trying to get things done and ticked off from their many lists.

Jo had the list for the salon opening party. Neva's mum, Dawn had the list for the engagement party, although that was a joint list with Judith, who was also involved in organising that event, as it was a party for her and Gavin too. Neva had the list for her wedding. That seemed to be the longest. And growing longer by the day.

Neva and Jo opened the door of The Mane Event at 9 on the 22nd. The day before had seen torrential rain, winds gusting at sixty miles per hour, and temperatures of well below average for February. They had seriously considered cancelling the open day, but the forecast promised fair weather for Saturday, and it hadn't been wrong. Warming rays of sunlight streamed through the glass frontage, and the gold balloons and fairy lights strung around the doors and windows, bobbed gently to and fro in a breeze as light as a hairdryer set on the lowest speed.

Rafe arrived shortly before 9 with the biggest bouquet of flowers Neva had ever seen, along with Ed, who had done the same. Neva and Jo didn't ask whose idea that had been and they both had to reapply their make-up before they opened.

Neva's family arrived next; Dawn and Rowan carried armfuls of containers crammed with cakes of all varieties, and Nigel and Dennis brought more champagne.

'It wouldn't do to run out,' Dennis said.

'You can never have enough champagne,' Rowan added.

'Now I'm almost nine,' said Sasha, 'I can have some, can't I?'

'No,' Nigel told her, but Rowan winked at him. 'OK. Maybe one teensy, tiny glass.'

Neva knew they'd probably give her lemonade and tell her it was champagne. Thankfully, Sasha had been persuaded to leave her puppy, Tempest at Dawn and Dennis' house.

'I wanted to bring him because he needs a haircut too,' Sasha said, and Rowan had to explain that dogs had their own, special hairdressing salons.

Cat, Amias, Kyra and Mary came next, and Neva introduced Rowan, Nigel and Sasha to Mary. She hoped they could discuss the possible purchase of Devon Villa, Cat having confirmed that Mary still intended to sell. She wasn't disappointed. Mary suggested the family might like to go and take a look around, but that Cat or Kyra would have to take them. She wasn't ready to set foot in Devon Villa again just yet. Not so soon after Jerusalem Raine's body had been removed from beneath the cellar floor.

'Was it all gooey, like an Egyptian mummy, or was it covered in blood?' Sasha asked, as Mary was about to take a bite out of a mini jam doughnut.

'We didn't see it,' Kyra told her, 'but we suspect it was mainly bones. She had been there for almost two hundred years and the flesh had no doubt rotted away.'

Mary had given a strangled cry and looked as if she were about to faint.

'Were there maggots and stuff?' Sasha asked, at which point, Neva told Rowan it might be best to intervene.

Judith and Gavin arrived next, along with Penny and Roger, and Wendy and Sean with their daughter, Taryn.

'The others are coming down later,' Judith said. 'And you may not believe this, but Olivia has demanded to come too. Adam and Hazel will be bringing her.'

'Olivia's coming here?' Suddenly Neva was nervous. One person she had never thought she'd see in her salon was Olivia Wynter. When Olivia had asked her the previous week, to do something with her hair in time for the weddings, Neva had assumed that would be at Wynter House.

'This will be the first time Olivia has ventured far from home in more years than I can recall,' said Rafe. 'Discounting her trip to hospital, of course.'

When Olivia did arrive, it was a bit like the Queen paying a visit. By then, some of the people from Merriment Bay had come to the opening, and everyone stood aside as Adam helped Olivia from his car and led her into the salon.

Olivia glanced around, took the proffered glass of champagne, and a seat on the multi-coloured sofa and announced that the place was just as she had expected. Neva wasn't sure if that was praise or condemnation, until she raised her glass in a toast and congratulated Neva and Jo on a great success.

Now it was Neva who almost fainted.

Olivia didn't stay long but to everyone's amazement, she did have a mini manicure ... and when Sasha returned with her parents after viewing Devon Villa, Olivia actually allowed Sasha to paint her nails, just because the child had said she wanted to.

There was one awkward moment when Cat and Kyra, along with Mary who had been persuaded to go to Devon Villa to show Rowan, Nigel and Sasha around, reappeared in the salon.

'Ah,' Olivia said. 'Good morning, Mary. It's been a long time since we met. I hear you're moving home, but let's not talk about that now, I assume these are Cat and Kyra, my granddaughter and great-granddaughter. Well, don't just stand there with your mouths open. Come and give me a kiss.'

'OK,' Neva said to Rafe. 'Who is this and where's the real Olivia?'

He beamed at her and kissed her on the lips after watching Cat and Kyra smile and do as Olivia said. 'This is because of you. You came to Wynter House and changed all our lives for the better.'

The day was a complete triumph. The salon was heaving for most of the day and by 3 p.m. Neva and Jo were having to turn people away. But they gave them discount vouchers and told them they were open from 9 a.m. on Monday.

Neva thought she would be too exhausted for the engagement party that night, but after a nap, a long soothing bath, and a relaxing, and rather sensual massage from Rafe, which turned into an hour of making love, she felt reinvigorated. She swept down the stairs of Wynter House on Rafe's arm, wearing a brand new and somewhat sexy, low cut, red evening gown. She also wore a necklace, bracelet and earrings that Olivia had given her as an engagement present.

'My darling Sebastian gave me these on our wedding day,' she said. 'I think it's only right that I give them to you today. He would be happy to see them worn by a beautiful young woman once again. And yes. I am saying I was beautiful in those days.'

Neva kissed her on her cheek. 'Thank you so much, Olivia. And you're beautiful now. Don't let anyone tell you otherwise. Not even a jumped-up hairdresser from Merriment Bay.'

Olivia smiled at her. 'I don't know any jumped-up hairdressers. But I do have a soon-to-be daughter-in-law who is a talented stylist. She did my hair for me today and I can't remember when I last looked this wonderful.'

Taryn sang, from a make-shift stage, and everyone danced, drank Wyntersleap Gin and Wyntersleap Gin cocktails, or champagne, and ate the magnificent selection of food provided by Penny, Wendy, Taryn, Dawn and Rowan.

Hazel and Adam danced for most of the night, but there was definitely some tension between them. Hazel had only returned for the day and would be going back to nurse her ex-boyfriend the following morning.

'Life is strange,' Adam said to Neva as he danced with her for one song. 'I never thought I'd fall in love, but when I do, the woman of my dreams goes back to nurse her ex. I have a feeling this love isn't going to last a lifetime, after all. And I really thought it might.'

'It might, Adam. Hazel's just doing her job. It doesn't mean she'll go back to her old relationship. Jo didn't when she had the chance. Rafe didn't. Maybe Hazel won't.'

'Maybe. But she told me this evening, when we had another, shall we say, disagreement, that this Jason guy needs her. He needs her much more than I do. She said I don't need anyone and never have.' He gave Neva the strangest look. 'That's not true, you know. I do need someone. I need Rafe. I know that sounds odd, but I do. Not in the way she meant, of course, but I've always wanted Rafe's approval. When I was younger, I wanted everything he had. But as I grew older and a little wiser, I realised I just wanted him to like me. And I realised he did and always had.'

'He loves you Adam. And so do I. But only as a soon-to-be sister-in-law. And don't get any ideas about us having an affair because that's never going to happen.' She laughed to make light of it.

'Damn,' he said. 'And I had such plans.' He laughed too. 'I'm so pleased Rafe and you are together. It proves that we can find true love. I hope I will, one day. I thought I had, but I think Hazel's true love lies somewhere else. I'll be fine though. As long as I have Rafe and you and Olivia and Wynter House.'

'You'll always have us, Adam. And you'll find someone. Now that you know what love is, you know what to look for if things don't work out for you and Hazel.'

And by the following day, it was fairly obvious they wouldn't.

'She said she still loves Jason,' Adam said when Hazel left just after breakfast. 'She said he needs her far more than I do, and that she loves being needed. She wants to be needed. She said she loves me too. It's just that she loves him more. I thought I might be having a heart attack when she told me, but it appears it's just heart break I'm feeling. Although Hazel called it hypertension or some such thing. I wasn't really listening by then.'

'I'm truly sorry,' Rafe said. 'I thought you'd found the one.'

'So did I. It seems I was wrong.'

Rafe nodded as he placed a hand on Adam's shoulder and smiled lovingly at Neva.

'There's someone out there for you, Adam. You just need to wait to find her.'

'I hope I don't have to wait as long as you did to find Neva. I'll be old and grey by then.'

'At least now you know what love is,' Olivia said, surprising everyone yet again with her empathy. 'Next time it'll be with the right girl. And there'll be another wedding at Wynter House. I can feel it in my bones.'

Chapter Thirty-One

The following weekend saw the official launch of Wyntersleap Gin, and to everyone's delight, the weather was perfect. Rafe, Sean and Adam had loved Neva's idea of the hot air balloon, and so it seemed did the press and potential buyers.

Kyra had agreed to do a photoshoot and had managed to rope in Francis Raine to go up in the balloon alongside her. They were both dressed in evening wear; Kyra in a beautiful emerald green, tightfitting gown that Cat said made her look much older than eighteen. Kyra's long ginger hair wafted in the gentle breeze, which had to be simulated by the large fans used to inflate the envelope because there wasn't a breath of wind today. Francis looked like a young James Bond and they were the epitome of the 'ideal' couple.

Kyra and Francis posed in the gondola of the balloon, each with a glass of Wyntersleap Gin in their hands and one of the gorgeous bottles fixed firmly in place beside them. It was a pale grey-blue bottle with what looked like splashes of water on the label and etched into the glass. The label had a white background with Wynter House at the top, looking exactly as it did, but in an illustrated form, and Wyntersleap Falls and River Wynter below it in shades of blue and white, looking just as magnificent as they did in reality. The words on the label read, 'Wyntersleap Gin. Distinctively dry gin from the waters of River Wynter.'

Kyra and Francis both said, 'Wyntersleap Gin is the perfect refreshment for high flyers,' as the balloon lifted smoothly off the ground and the videographer got excellent shots of the balloon and Wynter House and its grounds. Later, the videographer went up in the balloon with Kyra and Francis again and filmed Wyntersleap Falls in the background before panning down to film Merriment Bay with the sun over the sparkling waters of the bay. It couldn't have been a more idyllic looking scene if Rafe, Sean and Adam had paid a fortune for an expensive, commercial shoot.

Cat said she wasn't sure she liked her baby looking so grown up. It reminded her that Kyra was a woman. But Francis obviously liked what he saw. He couldn't take his eyes off Kyra all day.

After that, there was a delicious lunch, served in the dining room and then those members of the press, and any buyers who wanted to do so, were taken for a drive down to the village of Wyntersleap. They were also driven to the field leading to the Falls and some were daring enough to stand close to the edge. That was followed by afternoon tea, a visit to the distillery and then cocktails back at the house.

The launch was another successful day. Rafe, Sean and Adam got more orders than they thought possible, the press had nothing but praise for the gin, the tour, the vistas, the balloon, and the various repasts they were served. There were no accidents or mishaps, even though Sasha, along with her parents had been invited to the launch.

Although Sasha did tell one reporter that he looked a bit like a zombie. Amazingly, he took that as a compliment. He said he had a young daughter of his own who was into everything zombie-fied and he couldn't wait to tell her what Sasha had said.

'Some people are very strange,' Neva said to Rafe, as Ethel smacked her gums together and asked another reporter if he liked older women, before sucking on a chicken drumstick.

Chapter Thirty-Two

Grey Building & Design, the firm owned by Neva's sister and brother-in-law now that Dawn and Dennis had retired – or semi-retired, in Dennis' case, had been redecorating and repainting the cottages, the small shop and the Wyntersleap Inn in the village for a few weeks now. A couple of days before Judith and Gavin's wedding, Nigel and Dennis announced that the cottages, shop and pub were ready for the villagers to return.

Oddly enough, this news wasn't met with the shrieks of joy Nigel and Dennis had expected.

'I'll miss spending all day with my wife,' Roger said. 'Going back to run the shop each day while Penny works here will seem strange after all these weeks.'

'I'll miss helping out in the gardens and with the animals,' George said. 'My little cottage garden will seem very small again.'

'I'll miss the delicious meals,' said

Queenie. 'Oh not that your meals at the pub aren't wonderful, Wendy, because they are, but there's something special about sitting around a dining table with so many friendly faces.'

'We'll miss all the excitement,' Cecil and Ronnie said. 'Village life will seem rather dull compared to this. Although our dear Persephone will be thrilled to return to her own little patch of catnip in the garden of Ruby Cottage and watching all the birds in the trees nearby.'

'I'll miss watching Cecil and Ronnie listening at people's doors,' Ethel said, smacking her gums together. 'But I suppose they'll still do that in the village, won't you boys?'

Cecil and Ronnie tried to look affronted but they sniggered and nodded.

'At least it will be lovely to see Mabel and Lionel again,' Wendy said. 'And to hear all about their visit to Australia. I know it's the same every year. Lots of photos of their family and lots of stories about how wonderful Australia is, but it's a tradition now, and one to look forward to.'

'I'll miss spending my days in the distillery,' Sean said. 'Pulling pints in the pub and plugging in barrels of beer to the taps won't be as much fun as mixing herbs and other botanicals and coming up with new recipes for our gin.'

'You'll still spend some days here,' Wendy said. 'I'm perfectly capable of lifting and connecting barrels and pulling pints.'

'And Adam... speaking of pulling,' Ethel said. 'Did you see the photo of Mabel and Lionel's granddaughter? She's coming back with them, you know. She's a doctor and she's been offered a job at Eastbourne District Hospital. Looking at her picture, I'd say she could cure any ailment you might think you have. Including a broken heart.'

'Thanks, Ethel, but I think I need a bit of time before I start thinking about another relationship.' Adam laughed. 'Although I suppose it wouldn't hurt to take a look.'

'And she'll need someone to show her around,' Queenie said, grinning at Ethel. 'Show him the photo, Wendy.'

Wendy laughed and pulled out her phone, passing it across the dining table to Adam. He took the phone and raised his brows, a slow grin creeping across his face.

'Perhaps I don't need time, after all,' he said. 'Perhaps what I need is to get straight back on that horse.'

Ethel cackled. 'Don't let Mabel hear you call her granddaughter a horse, young Adam.' Although it was clear she knew exactly what he had meant.

Neva looked at Rafe and Rafe nodded.

'Neva and I have discussed this,' Rafe said,

'together with Adam and with Olivia's blessing, and while we agree that it's right that you should all return to your homes and to your own lives, a house this size should always be filled with guests. So, assuming you all want to, we're suggesting you all come here to Wynter House and stay for at least one weekend each month. Or more often, if you like. That way, you'll still have the privacy of your own homes, but the pleasure of gatherings such as this. It's entirely up to each and every one of you, of course. Please don't feel obligated in any way to come and stay.'

'Obligated?' Ethel said. 'Put my name down for each and every one of those weekends.'

'Mine too,' said Queenie. 'Can I still bring Boris and Duchess?'

'Yes,' Rafe said. 'But the same rules will apply. No dogs in the dining room.'

'Does this include us?' Cecil asked, still clearly finding it hard to believe they'd been welcomed into the fold.

'Of course,' said Rafe. 'And yes, Persephone too, before you ask. And if George wants to spend some more time here, I'm going to ask him if he and Gavin can build some sort of outside run for Persephone. That way you won't have to walk her around the corridors of the house.'

'I'll happily do that,' George said, beaming.

'Oh thank you, Rafe. And thank you, George,' Cecil said, clapping his hands together.

Everyone else said they too wanted to come and stay.

'Although what do we do about the pub?' Wendy said.

'We could close it for those weekends, Mum,' Taryn suggested. 'Most of our regulars would be here anyway. Or we could employ some temporary staff just for the odd weekend here and there.'

'And we could do the same with our shop,' Penny said. 'It's not as if we get that many customers from elsewhere.'

'That's settled then,' Rafe said. 'I'm sure we can make this work well for all of us. But there's really no point in you all rushing to your homes until after Judith and Gavin's, and Neva and my weddings, is there? I mean, we'll all have enough to do without having to worry about moving furniture back and forth.'

'I'm not sure you really want to see them go at all,' Neva said.

Rafe grinned at her. 'To be honest, I'm not sure either. I've got used to having them all at Wynter House.'

Chapter Thirty-Three

'Life at Wynter House is beginning to feel as it did when I was a young bride, living here,' Olivia said, as they sat at the dining table for Judith and Gavin's wedding breakfast. 'A stream of parties and celebrations.'

'Olivia does have a point,' Rafe said.

What with the salon opening and the engagement party, Rafe's launch party, now Judith and Gavin's wedding, and next weekend, Neva and Rafe's, it did feel as if champagne corks were popping non-stop.

Judith looked beautiful in an ivory, satin dress. It was a simple creation with a boat neck, long sleeves and a plain flowing gown, not too tightly fitted. She wore a short veil, and a small, diamond tiara Olivia lent her as her 'something borrowed'. Olivia had also lent one to Neva, but it was bigger and had been the one Olivia had worn to her own wedding.

'Be thankful I didn't give you my wedding dress to wear,' Olivia said. 'Not that you would fit into it. I was slimmer than you when I married.'

'Er. Thank you, Olivia,' Neva said. 'The tiara is beautiful. I'll be proud to wear it.'

The ceremony in the chapel was short. Judith and Gavin exchanged vows but they didn't write their own. They just used the standard version.

After that, they had an afternoon tea, followed by dancing, where once again, Taryn performed. And later, in the early evening, a formal dinner of eight courses.

Judith and Gavin left for the Lake District the following morning, after spending their wedding night in Wynter House. But not in Judith's own room. Olivia insisted on having one of the other rooms aired for them.

The wedding day was magical – but not as magical as Neva and Rafe's.

Their day dawned with sunshine and a gentle breeze, unseasonably warm weather and not a cloud in the sky. Perfect weather for the marquees set up in the grounds at the front and sides of Wynter House.

The chapel was festooned with flowers of a multitude of colours. Neva wanted this to be a bright and joyous occasion. Rafe looked more handsome than ever in a grey morning suit, top hat and tails and a pale blue tie to match the pale blue ribbon that was threaded through Neva's hair, and repeated in her veil.

Neva's dress was white coarse silk with a sweetheart neckline, three-quarter-length sleeves, and an A-line gown, which was just as well as Neva seemed to have put on weight with all the celebrations. Her mum and Jo had to struggle to do up the many silk-covered tiny buttons down the back of the dress.

'Happiness is making you fat,' Jo said.

'Says the woman who spends all her time in the local fish and chip shop.'

'But not eating fish and chips,' Jo said with a satisfied sigh and a wink.

The chapel was small so only family and close friends attended the wedding. Jo, Rowan, and Sasha, along with Cat and Kyra were bridesmaids and although Sasha had wanted to wear her Zombie Princess dress, she was persuaded to wear the pale blue satin dress, along with matching shoes. She even wore a ring of flowers in her hair. She looked so pretty that Rowan broke down in tears. Twice.

The Reverend Raine officiated and Neva and Rafe proclaimed the vows they had written themselves.

Neva's were about a family Christmas break leading to being flooded out and meeting the love of her life.

Rafe's were about the fact that True Love could change people and that Wynter House looked and felt so much more beautiful since Neva had come to stay.

The wedding feast was held in one of the marquees, with dancing in the other. The only tiny disappointment of the day was that Hazel didn't attend. She sent a gift and a letter saying that she felt it was for the best as she didn't want Adam to be upset. She also sent a text saying she hoped she and Jo and Neva could still all be friends although she realised that may not be possible.

'Of course it is,' Neva had replied. 'But we won't meet up at Wynter House.'

Jo caught the bouquet when Neva threw it and although she had said she didn't want to get married, she smiled and later told Neva that if Olivia Wynter could change, then so could Jo Duncan. Especially now that the right man might have come into her life.

Neva and Rafe danced all night. They, like Judith and Gavin were spending their wedding night at Wynter House, but in Rafe's room.

'I want our marriage to start off in the same bed where we'll spend so many of our nights together for the rest of our lives,' Neva said, when she and Rafe had discussed it, two days before their wedding.

'Not all our nights?' Rafe queried. 'Are you planning to spend some nights in Merriment Bay at the flat with Jo?'

'Of course I'm not. But even though we may not have much money now, perhaps we will go away in the future.'

He laughed and breathed a sigh of relief.

'Actually, I've got a little surprise,' he said, but he refused to tell her until after they were married.

'So what's this surprise then?' Neva asked as they danced at the reception.

Rafe beamed at her. 'We're going away tomorrow. Just for a few days. Ed told me about a rather nice hotel in Majorca and his friend happens to know the owner. He managed to get us the honeymoon suite and Adam's paid for it all as our wedding present.'

'Oh Rafe,' Neva said, reaching up and throwing her arms around his neck.

She immediately regretted that, when several tiny silk buttons popped off the back of her dress and shot across the room, but she didn't care. Until Olivia gave her the strangest look.

'Am I correct in thinking this may not be the last celebration we'll be having at Wynter House, or the last time our chapel will be used in the near future?'

Neva didn't understand at first and nor did Rafe.

'Adam will hopefully marry there,' Rafe said.

'Don't be a fool, Rafe,' Olivia laughed. 'I mean long before that day happens.'

'Cat and Amias, you mean?' Neva said.

Olivia gave her another strange look. 'I

hadn't even considered that. Amias Wells marrying in our chapel?' She gave a tiny shrug. 'Well, I suppose one must learn to accept situations one cannot change. And he does seem rather a decent, pleasant young man, so yes, that's a possibility. But are you telling me, Neva that you don't know? Hmm. And I thought you were a bright young woman. I'm not talking about a wedding at Wynter House. I'm talking about a christening.'

'A christening?' Neva and Rafe stared at one another and then stared at Neva's slightly visible, rounded tummy. 'A christening!'

'Oh my God!' Neva said. 'I can't be. I'm on the pill.'

'You had that Norovirus over New Year,' Jo reminded her, as she returned one of the buttons. 'They say the pill doesn't always work if you've got sickness and diarrhoea. And from what I remember you telling me, you definitely had quite a lot of both.'

Neva gasped before looking a little nervously at Rafe but she couldn't hide the thrill and excitement she felt.

'I think Olivia may be right. I thought I was late due to the stress and excitement of all the events we've had and I put the feelings of nausea down to nerves.'

Rafe's eyes filled with love and laughter and pure bliss.

'Are you saying what I think you're saying?'

He could hardly speak as he took her in his arms.

'Of course she is,' Olivia said.

'Are you OK with this?' Neva asked him.

'OK?' He threw his head back and laughed. 'No. I'm not OK. I'm overjoyed. I'm euphoric. I'm the happiest man in the world.'

'What's going on?' Adam asked, another button in his hand.

Neva and Rafe were too busy kissing to respond.

'We're going to be welcoming another Wynter to Wynter House, Adam,' Olivia said, as proud as punch. 'I'm going to be a great-grandmother ... again. And I couldn't be happier. Carruthers! Bring us more champagne. And bring one for yourself. We've got something even more wonderful than a wedding at Wynter House to celebrate!'

Coming soon

Wedding Bells in Merriment Bay

See my website for details.

A Note from Emily

Thank you for reading this book. A little piece of my heart goes into all of my books and when I send them on their way, I really hope they bring a smile to someone's face. If this book made you smile, or gave you a few pleasant hours of relaxation, I'd love it if you would tell your friends.

I'd be really happy if you have a minute or two to post a review. Just a line will do, and a kind review makes such a difference to my day – to any author's day. Huge thanks to those of you who do so, and for your lovely comments and support on social media. Thank you.

A writer's life can be lonely at times. Sharing a virtual cup of coffee or a glass of wine, or exchanging a few friendly words on Facebook, Twitter or Instagram is so much fun.

You might like to join my Readers' Club by signing up for my newsletter. It's absolutely free, your email address is safe and won't be shared and I won't bombard you, I promise. You can enter competitions and enjoy some giveaways. In addition to that, there's my author page on Facebook and there's also a new Facebook group. You can chat with me and with other fans and get access to my book news, snippets from my daily life, early extracts from my books and lots more besides. Details are on the 'For You' page of my website. You'll find all my contact links in the Contact section following this.

I'm working on my next book right now. Let's see where my characters take us this time. Hope to chat with you soon.

To see details of my other books, please go to the books page on my website, or scan the QR code below to see all my books on Amazon.

Contact

If you want to be the first to hear Emily's news, find out about book releases, enter competitions and gain automatic entry into her Readers' Club, go to: https://www.emilyharvale.com and subscribe to her newsletter via the 'Sign me up' box. If you love Emily's books and want to chat with her and other fans, ask to join the exclusive Emily Harvale's Readers' Club Facebook group.

Or come and say 'Hello' on Facebook, Twitter and Instagram.

Contact Emily via social media:
www.twitter.com/emilyharvale
www.facebook.com/emilyharvalewriter
www.facebook.com/emilyharvale
www.instagram.com/emilyharvale

Or by email via the website:
www.emilyharvale.com

Acknowledgements

My grateful thanks go to the following:

Christina Harkness for her patience and care in editing this book.

My webmaster, David Cleworth who does so much more than website stuff.

My cover design team, JR.

Luke Brabants. Luke is a talented artist and can be found at: www.lukebrabants.com

My wonderful friends for their friendship and love. You know I love you all.

All the fabulous members of my Readers' Club. You help and support me in so many ways and I am truly grateful for your ongoing friendship. I wouldn't be where I am today without you.

My Twitter and Facebook friends, and fans of my Facebook author page. It's great to chat with you. You help to keep me (relatively) sane! Thank you for buying this book.